TANGLED WATERS
ENCHANTED WATERS

JENNA ST. JAMES
STEPHANIE DAMORE

Tangled Waters

Jenna St. James

&

Stephanie Damore

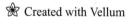 Created with Vellum

"Happy one-month anniversary, Isla," Kyra Hayes said as I strolled through the front door of Seashell Sweets Bakery. "Your usual?"

"My usual sounds great," I said to the beautiful sea witch, who was fast becoming my friend. I'd made it a point to stop in at the bakery every morning since moving to Neptune Oasis, and being a creature of habit, I always ordered the same thing.

After the fifth day, Kyra knew what to expect.

My mom was a mermaid, and my dad had been a sea witch. Water was my magical element...which was why I loved coming to Seashell Sweets Bakery. Just stepping through the front doors filled me with a sense of serenity. The walls were adorned with delicate seashell motifs and murals of gentle waves. The floor, designed to mimic the sandy beaches found in the Bermuda Triangle, transitioned from a light tan near the entrance to a soothing teal as customers walked toward the display case. Pink and teal chairs with wave-patterned cushions were placed near one wall so customers could sit and enjoy their treats while the ambient sounds of soft waves and distant seagulls played in the background. The tables and chairs in front of the windows were also fashioned in the same pastel pink and teal design.

The display counter, made of a translucent material reminiscent of frosted sea glass, showcased an array of mostly ocean-themed pastries that seemed too beautiful to eat. But my favorite accent pieces were the four off-white chandeliers made of seashells, pearls, and teardrop crystals.

Kyra smiled at me over the display case, and the cluster of stars tattooed across her temple sparkled like diamonds. Because they were magically enhanced, the stars changed colors on their own. "One cinnamon-vanilla latte and a rosewater madeleine coming up."

One month ago, the Paranormal Apprehension & Detention Agency sent me and my grandmother, Nana, to the Bermuda Triangle. We were to figure out who was after the infamous fertility stone that had been lost at sea when the *Sea Venture* went down back in the 1600s. An anonymous tip had come in to PADA headquarters that treasure hunters were asking questions on the Bermuda Triangle islands, and so the Cursed Artifact Recovery Division sent Nana and me to find the fertility stone before the treasure hunters could get their hands on it.

While on Neptune Oasis—the largest of the three islands that made up the Bermuda Triangle—I'd run into former PADA detective and long-time friend, Shayla Loci-Stone. She'd been honeymooning on the island with her husband, Alex Stone. It used to be humans stayed away from the tropical paradise of Bermuda because they feared the strange and unexplainable incidents that happened—which was exactly how supernaturals wanted it, and why they perpetuated the rumors and scare tactics. But over the years, humans had thrown caution to the wind and started vacationing more and more in Bermuda. Now the local supernaturals had to cloak the cluster of islands so the humans didn't discover magic—giving the humans Bermuda, and the supernaturals the Bermuda Triangle.

"Good morning, Detective Ceartas," octopus shifter Celia Bromley said as she sidled up next to me. "It's a quiet Wednesday morning on the island."

"It is," I agreed. "Beautiful and quiet."

Celia smiled. "And that's why Sheriff Sebastian stayed at his job for as long as he did."

Two weeks ago, the Bermuda Triangle's sheriff, Sebastian Logger, suddenly retired. Now the three islands that made up the Bermuda Triangle—Neptune Oasis, Spring Island, and Sapphire Isle—were without law enforcement of any kind. Since Nana and I were nomads at heart, PADA convinced us to make the Bermuda Triangle our home base for an undisclosed amount of time.

And so far...Nana and I were loving it. The weather was perfect, the crime rate was almost non-existent, and I could swim the ocean waters whenever I wanted—a huge perk for a mermaid sea witch like myself. Even Nana was getting into the swing of PADA retirement by volunteering to be the dispatcher and secretary at the tiny hut that housed the newly renovated Bermuda Triangle PADA Station.

"You're in early," Kyra said as she took out a beautifully decorated madeleine from the display case. "What's the occasion?"

"I don't have to clock in until nine, so I thought I'd get an early start since I have a list of things I still need for the bungalow Nana and I share."

"Most places on the island don't open until eight," Kyra said, her short jet-black hair gleaming under the chandelier lights. "And it's only seven now."

3

I smiled. "Guess that means I can sit and relax with a coffee and one of your beautiful madeleines and people watch."

Kyra's madeleines were genuine works of art. Cake-like seashells dipped in green, blue, or pink icing and then dipped in edible glitter, pearls, or flowers. I almost hated devouring the delicious mini cakes.

Almost.

"Before I forget, Detective Ceartas," Celia said, "I wanted to invite you to a singles meet-and-greet. It's for ages thirty-five to fifty-five."

"Well, at forty, I guess I qualify," I joked. "And you can call me Isla."

Celia dug around in her purse and handed me a flyer. "Here ya go, Isla. No pressure. Just thought you might like to meet others your age since you're new to the island."

I thanked her as she turned and headed for a table near the window.

"You going?" I asked, waving the flyer in front of me.

"I don't know," Kyra said. "I mean, I *can* since I'm thirty-eight and single. Thanks to the divorce." She snorted. "But I'm just not sure I'm ready to meet anyone yet. I feel I should focus on the bakery and Maddy. She's a senior this year and already talking about college."

"Really?" I mused. "Does she know where?"

"She's looking at a supernatural culinary school in North Carolina." She gestured to the exquisite madeleine she'd set out for me. "This recipe was hers."

"Really?" I mused. "Well, it's divine. My absolute favorite. Next to the chocolate ganache madeleine and the carrot cake madeleine and the chai madeleine." I grinned. "You know I could go on forever, right?"

Kyra laughed and slid my cinnamon-vanilla latte across the

counter, then leaned in conspiratorially. "Are you any closer to finding your fertility stone?"

I shook my head and snatched up the coffee. "Not yet. But I'm hopeful."

Thanking her, I picked up the plastic seashell plate with my pink rosewater madeleine and snagged a table near a window overlooking the busy street. I spent the next few minutes eating my delicious cake-like cookie and sipping my latte.

With Samhain only a week away, the storefronts were decorating their windows for the holiday season. Some windows were decorated in traditional fall colors with pumpkins and typical fall décor, while others went for a more gothic and spookier look. My favorite was the skeleton outside Triton's Treasures—a supernatural antiques store. The owner had spelled the skeleton to joke with tourists and locals as they walked by and lure them inside the shop.

I was almost finished with my early morning breakfast when the front door to the bakery opened, and Jace Solari and his snarky talking dragon, Glo, entered the shop. Jace was a demigod. An actual descendant of the Greek god, Apollo.

Tall, broad-shouldered, and drop-dead gorgeous with his dark hair and chiseled jaw...I hated the thrill I got every time I saw him.

Jace Solari was bad news.

Shayla Loci-Stone had informed me before she left the island that the arrogant demigod had snatched a gold coin out of the ocean, and I was bound and determined to get it back from the mischievous thief.

Jace's sea-green eyes locked on me, and he grinned when he caught me staring. I stifled a groan as he strode my way. The demigod stood for everything I despised—a self-serving treasure hunter looking out for only himself and his next big score.

Just like my mother.

Or so I believed.

When I was just weeks from turning sixteen, my mother left on one of her aquatic treasure hunts. She'd promised to return before my birthday…but it never happened. In fact, I never saw my mother again. I was sure she came to a bad end, but since I didn't have definitive proof, a part of me always hoped she'd be found alive.

Of course, that would mean she *purposely* didn't return, but at least knowing would give Nana and me closure.

I never knew my dad. According to my mom, he was just another treasure seeker like her. When he found out Mom was pregnant, he told her he didn't want to be tied down with a kid. So Mom went back to Nana's house on one of the tiny Hebridean islands off the coast of Scotland and gave birth to me. But like the man who'd fathered me…my mom had no desire to give up treasure hunting. And so for most of my childhood, Mom would pop in and out of my life, leaving Nana to raise me on one of the cluster of Hebridean islands—that is, when Nana wasn't off on a PADA assignment herself.

I knew it broke Nana's heart that my mom never followed in her footsteps and used her mermaid talents to help PADA relocate cursed artifacts…which was why I'd worked so hard to get into PADA and become a detective. I'd never had the desire to hunt treasure—mainly because it left a bitter taste in my mouth —but when Nana started showing signs of forgetting important facts and dates, I didn't hesitate to change divisions so I could help her safeguard her precious cursed artifacts.

"Good morning, Detective Ceartas," Jace said, stopping next to my table.

I picked up my coffee and quickly gulped down the hot liquid in hopes he'd take the hint and leave me alone—then nearly spat the liquid back out when it burned my mouth.

"You okay?" he asked, amusement dancing in his eyes.

"I'm fine," I lied. "You ready to give me back the gold coin you illegally stole weeks ago from a sunken pirate ship?"

Jace held up his hands and grinned. "You can search me right now, Detective. I promise you, I don't have it."

The diminutive dragon, barely bigger than a hummingbird, cackled and landed on Jace's shoulder. "Yeah, Fishy Witch. We don't have your gold coin."

I rolled my eyes, accustomed to her snarky remarks. Being part sea witch, I wasn't exactly on Glo's list of favorite people. After all, it was a sea witch who'd captured her, spelled her with the ability to speak, and then turned her dragon scales into their current color-changing, glow-in-the-dark state.

Jace told me "Glo" was short for Gloria, but I thought it was more in line with the fact the tiny dragon had the unique ability to glow-in-the-dark at night. During the day, her scales and wings change colors with her mood—which meant the snarky scowler spent a lot of time in black and gray and red. But once the sun sank below the horizon, she glowed like the luminescent sea creatures that swam in the depths of the ocean.

Glo shrugged. "You don't have to worry about me stealing any silly coin, Fishy Witch." She reached down with one of her front claws and snatched the tiny flask she kept strapped around her body in a purple sling, uncorked it, and took a healthy swig. "I have better things to do with my time. Thank you very much."

I ignored the dragon's attempt to rile me. "That's Detective Ceartas to you, Glo."

Glo smacked her lips, capped the flask, and dropped it against her green and purple scales. "Oh, excuse me? Did I hit a nerve?"

"I'd like to finish my breakfast in peace," I said. "So I'd appreciate it if you both left me alone."

Jace smiled and slid his hands inside his jeans pockets. "I actually came over to see if you'd be a character witness for me. You know, in case my charge of Diving in Protected Waters actually goes to trial."

I knew for a fact Jace had stolen the gold coin—I just couldn't prove it beyond a shadow of a doubt. But I'd been able to arrest him for Diving in Protected Waters based on the testimony of Shayla Loci-Stone, Alex Stone, and Hydra Ann—the kraken who lived in the ocean between two of the islands. By having Jace arrested, it also forced him to stay on the island where I needed him. I was bound and determined to get that gold coin and turn it into PADA's Cursed Artifact Recovery team.

"A character witness?" I mused. "Really? I don't think so." I shrugged. "Besides, the way I heard it, you and your attorney, Fredrick Longshore, had a rather loud falling out the other day. I think the rumor was you called the barracuda shifter some not-so-kind names."

"Trust me," Jace said, "it wasn't anything the lawyer hadn't heard before."

"You're probably right." I stood and brushed fallen crumbs onto my seashell plate. "But I'm afraid I'm still going to pass on being a character witness for you. I'm already a witness for the prosecution."

"I doubt your charges will stick," Jace said.

I shrugged. "Maybe. Maybe not. Hope your lawyer isn't one to hold a grudge, Mr. Solari. I'd hate to think you wouldn't get a fair trial."

"Call me Jace." He winked at me. "And I doubt it goes to trial."

"Do you know something I don't?" I mused, pushing in my chair.

Before Jace could answer, my cell phone rang. I glanced down at the display and smiled. It was Nana.

"Hey, Nana," I said into the phone. "What's up?"

"Just got a call from the retired sheriff about a dead body," she said. "He said it was out by Bone Reef, wherever that is."

"Bone Reef?" I mused.

Jace's eyes widened. "I know where Bone Reef is. There's not much out there."

I scowled and lowered the phone. "I don't need your help, Mr. Solari. I'm sure I can find it on my own."

He shrugged. "Suit yourself."

"Yeah," Glo echoed, her scales and wings glowing red. "Suit yourself."

"I'll be there in five minutes," I said to Nana.

"Better make it twenty," Jace said. "Bone Reef is on the north side of Neptune Oasis."

I scowled at the demigod before turning my back on him and speaking into the phone. "I'll be there in fifteen minutes, Nana."

2

Since most of the vehicles on the three islands that made up the Bermuda Triangle consisted of golf carts, tiny trucks, mini-coopers, mopeds, motorcycles, and bicycles, getting somewhere fast was almost impossible. Add in that the terrain on the north side of Neptune Oasis was rocky and dangerous, it was more like thirty minutes before I pulled my brand new off-road Polaris Pro XD to a stop next to the former sheriff's S-10 truck.

"Hope it's okay I'm here," the former sheriff said as he lumbered out of his truck. "I still get calls from the locals."

"I appreciate any help I can get, Sheriff Sebastian," I said honestly.

"It's just Sebastian now," the elderly crab shifter said. "I did my time."

I chuckled. "Understood. So what do we have?"

Sebastian sighed and ran a large, weathered hand over his face. "It's bad, Detective Ceartas."

"Isla," I said.

He nodded. "Isla. The two brothers who found the body are down the path there. No surprise, they're pretty shaken up. Do you want to see the body first or talk to the young teens first?"

"Let's see the body," I said.

We carefully navigated the rocky ground, trying our best to keep our footing as we made our way down the side of the cliff. Bermuda cedars, palmettos, and yellow wood trees clung to the rugged terrain, their roots tightly gripping the soil between the rocks. The ocean breeze carried the scent of salt, sea life, and the tang of algae from the shoreline below.

As we ventured closer, my trained eyes caught the subtle play of colors in the breeze. It was a soft, mesmerizing dance of purples and aqua. Magic swirled around the scene, drawing us closer. I slowed as we approached.

"He's right over there," Sebastian said, nodding toward the colors.

"Yeah, I see him. The colors are drawing me in."

"What's that now?" Sebastian hitched up his pants.

"The colors. You don't see them? It's almost like a haze in the air."

Sebastian cocked his head.

"Wait a second," I inched my way closer, quickly realizing why the crab shifter probably wasn't picking up on the magical trail. "It's mermaid magic."

Most supernaturals could detect what type of supernatural another person was. Maybe not completely. It could be they were a mixed species like me, or they were a normal—a supernatural who was born without the ability to perform magic or shift. But for the most part, supernaturals could sense the different species.

"That explains it," Sebastian said. "I got no mermaid ancestry in me, believe it or not."

I peered down at the dead body. The unidentified man was lying on his side, his face buried deep in the sand, and his hands and feet bound with charmed seaweed. An enchanted net of swirling hues covered his body. At first, I thought the net was made of rope, but on closer inspection, I wasn't sure. I didn't dare touch it to find out.

"What do we know about the victim?" I asked, taking a step back to examine the surrounding area.

"Fredrick Longshore," Sebastian said. "He was an attorney for the unsavory, so to speak. He has an office on Splash Island."

"What?" I turned and faced Sebastian. "That's Fredrick Longshore in the net? Being facedown, I didn't recognize him."

"I've known him my whole life," Sebastian said. "I knew who he was the minute I saw him."

It took me less than a week living in the Bermuda Triangle to know who Fredrick Longshore was and the reputation he had on the three islands. And given his history, the suspect list would be a mile long–starting with Jace Solari.

"No next-of-kin to report to," Sebastian said. "His parents died years ago, and he never had any children. Has an ex-wife, but she isn't entitled to know. Rumor has it he's dating Missy Weiss now. She owns Pearls & Pendants downtown."

"Is Doc Bowers on her way?" I asked.

Sebastian nodded. "She is. I called her immediately after I called dispatch."

I smiled at that. Dispatch was just Nana, but the retired sheriff refused to call her anything other than "dispatch" no matter how hard I tried to get him to do otherwise.

"Doc Bowers and the new forensics guy should be here any minute now," Sebastian said.

When I'd first arrived on the island, there'd been no forensic scientist, and the medical examiner only had an office on Splash

Island. When I'd agreed to take the position, PADA immediately looked for a forensic scientist. They'd hired Neil Thatcher, a hulking crocodile shifter.

"Then let's get to work processing the scene," I said. "You don't mind helping, do you?"

"Not at all." He pulled out two sets of gloves from his back pocket and handed me a pair.

We bent down and carefully examined the netting Fredrick Longshore was ensnared in. The powerful magic emanating off the netting made me pause. I thought I could diffuse it, but I wasn't sure.

"Whaddya thinking?" Sebastian asked.

"I could do a counter spell," I said. "But I don't have a pearl."

"Got ya covered." Sebastian reached inside his pants pocket and yanked out a cream-colored pearl. "What else do you need?"

"Saltwater and a seashell."

Bending down, he picked up a seashell off the sand. "Let me fill this for you."

As he lumbered down to the water, I continued to study what I could see of the barracuda shifter who'd once been Fredrick Longshore. Even though his hands and feet were bound by magically enhanced seaweed, there were no other visible wounds I could see.

When Sebastian returned, he handed me the seashell he'd filled with saltwater from the ocean. Placing the pearl in the middle of the water-filled shell, I closed my eyes and whispered the spell that would counter the magic rolling off the net. As the magic slowly dissipated, I heard a commotion off in the distance.

Medical examiner, Brystal Bowers, was a true dichotomy.

The tall, dark-haired necromancer with her hippie-like attire and perpetual smile always brought with her an air of positivity, even in the face of death.

"Morning blessings, all!" Doc Bowers said, her voice as cheery as her outfit. "What's the magical word?"

I managed a faint smile.

"We've got a body, Doc," Sebastian said. "Fredrick Longshore."

Doc Bowers whistled. "This won't be an easy one to solve." She squatted down and examined the body. "Mermaid magic, if I'm not mistaken." She looked up at us and grinned. "I'm an eighth mermaid on my Mama's side."

I nodded. "Yeah, I picked up on the mermaid magic myself." I turned and greeted the new forensic scientist as he sidled up to me. "Hey, Neil."

"Detective Ceartas."

Despite his human appearance, there was an undeniable primal energy about the crocodile shifter, as if the raw strength of his crocodile still pulsed beneath his skin. He'd carried his forensics collection kit with him, so I backed up to let him, Sebastian, and Doc Bowers get to work.

"Well, let's have a look-see, shall we?" Doc Bowers chirped, her enthusiasm undiminished by the somber circumstances.

As the three began their meticulous examination of the scene, I turned my attention to the two brothers who stood a little distance away, huddled together as if seeking comfort from each other.

I sauntered over to where they stood. Both boys looked like they were on the verge of fleeing, glancing over their shoulders as if they expected trouble any second. Their faces held a mix of fear, curiosity, and guilt. I approached them with a friendly smile, hoping to put them at ease.

"Hey, there," I began, my tone gentle. "I'm Detective Ceartas. I'd like to ask you a few questions about what you found. Is that all right?"

The taller of the two, who seemed to be the older brother, nodded hesitantly. "Um, yeah, sure. We didn't do anything wrong, though."

The younger brother elbowed his older brother, his eyes wide.

"Well, not really," the older brother amended.

"What do you mean by that?" I asked curiously.

"We're supposed to be in school," the older boy said. "But we're not missing nothing. Mrs. Slimebottom is covering reefs in lecture today, and we know all about those."

"Yeah," the younger brother piped up, his hair changing from yellow to a vibrant green before transitioning to blue. "We know all about those."

"Cuttlefish shifters?" I guessed, taking in the boy's changing colors.

"Yes, ma'am," the older brother confirmed.

I offered them an understanding nod. "I'm not here to get you in trouble for skipping school. I'm focused on something much more important right now." I ignored their shifting hair, the colors changing as if reflecting their emotions. "Can you tell me your names?"

The older brother spoke up again, his voice a touch more steady now. "I'm Jeremy, and this is my little brother, Jordan."

"Nice to meet you both. Like I said, I'm Detective Isla Ceartas."

"Does your name mean something?" Jeremy asked.

I nodded. "Isla is said like 'island' but without the ending sound, and my last name is Gaelic for justice."

"Cool," the boys said simultaneously.

"I'm not here to bust you for skipping," I said. "We're just trying to piece together what happened. You're the ones who called the police?"

Jeremy swallowed, his expression serious. "I did. We were walking along the trail, you know, trying to kill time. We almost tripped over him. I couldn't believe it."

Jordan shivered, his eyes wide as he looked toward the crime scene. "Yeah, it was like something out of a book or a movie. We couldn't believe our eyes."

I nodded. "I bet. Did you notice anyone else walking or hiking around here?"

"No, ma'am," Jeremy answered. "We haven't seen no one around here."

Jordan nodded. "That's true. We haven't seen no one."

"And did you touch anything or disturb the scene in any way?"

The boys shook their heads emphatically, their hair changing color once again.

I wasn't surprised. The brothers had mostly been in the wrong place at the wrong time. If anything, maybe the macabre discovery would discourage them from skipping school again. "I'm sorry you had to see what you did today, but thank you for talking with me."

They both nodded, their fear gradually giving way to relief.

After letting the boys go, I turned and made my way back to the crime scene where Doc Bowers and Neil were deep in their work. Sebastian stood off to the side.

"I don't know the boys," I said. "I told them I wouldn't bust their chops for skipping, but maybe someone should be informed?"

Sebastian grinned. "I know the boys' parents. Busted the dad myself a time or two for skipping when he was a boy. I'll go see the parents later."

"Thanks." I turned to where Doc Bowers was working. "Any news?"

Doc Bowers looked up from her examination, a frown tugging at her usually upbeat expression. "It's a complicated mess, Isla. The use of mermaid magic is making it nearly impossible to determine the time of death. I might get something more concrete when I get him on the table, but you may have to rely on other evidence to piece things together."

Nodding, I turned to Neil. "Any clues that might lead us to who killed him?"

Neil's eyes were focused, his expression thoughtful. "Not yet, but I'll make sure we examine every inch of this place."

I nodded. "Thanks, Neil."

Fredrick Longshore's connection to the Bermuda Triangle and the magical net that enveloped him hinted at a personal connection. Someone had used mermaid magic to cloak his death…a deliberate attempt to complicate our investigation.

With the brothers unable to provide any direct leads, it seemed finding out who the last person to see Fredrick alive would be crucial. I leaned against a nearby rock, watching as the waves crashed against the shore below.

As Doc Bowers and Neil worked to carefully move the body, my attention was briefly pulled away by an uneasy feeling prickling at the back of my neck. It was that familiar sixth sense I'd developed over the years. The feeling that someone was watching me. My instincts kicked in, and I turned my head to scan the surroundings.

And there, standing at the ledge of the cliff, was Jace Solari. He leaned casually against the rocky outcrop, his gaze fixed on me. His presence always seemed to bring an air of tension and suspicion. What was he doing here? And why was he watching me? I met his gaze with a guarded expression, my detective's intuition telling me that his appearance was no coincidence.

3

"What are you doing here, Jace?" I demanded as I strode over to him.

"Just making sure you got here safely," he said.

I narrowed my eyes. "Do you know whose body is down there?"

"No. Why would I?"

"Because it's your attorney. You know, the one you had a fight with recently?"

Jace threw back his head and laughed. "You can't *seriously* think I killed him?"

"Yeah," Glo said, her wings glowing red. "That man was a barracuda. Literally. Lots of people hated him."

I arched a brow at the dragon. "Really? And how would you know?"

"Because," Jace said, "Glo and I heard him arguing with someone on the phone right before my meeting with him." He grinned. "You know, the one where we got into a fight."

"Who was Fredrick arguing with?" I asked.

"Someone named Chester." He shrugged. "I didn't care to listen, but from the shouting, it sounded serious. Maybe you should ask Fredrick's secretary. She heard the argument. Her name is Celeste Zephyr."

I nodded, mentally noting down the information. Jace's nonchalant attitude might be a façade, but his words were adding a new layer to the puzzle. If Fredrick had been arguing with someone named Chester, it could provide a lead.

"All right," I said, my gaze still fixed on Jace. "I'll look into that."

Jace smiled. "You do that, Detective."

"But since you're here, why don't you tell me where you were last night from eight until six this morning?"

Jace's smile remained in place, though I could sense a touch of tension in his stance. "Glo and I were home."

I held his gaze, studying his expression for any signs of deception. "Just the two of you? All night?"

He nodded, his gaze steady. "That's right."

Glo fluttered her wings impatiently, her scales pulsating with a deep shade of red. "You heard him, Witch. We were at home, minding our own business."

"I'm only half sea witch," I pointed out.

"Fishy Witch!" Glo hissed.

I suppressed a sigh, not entirely convinced of Jace's innocence. Just like with the gold coin. "Fine. But don't think that clears you of suspicion."

He shrugged. "Trust me, Detective. I've got nothing to hide."

"Uh-huh, just like you didn't steal that gold coin?"

"What coin?" Jace winked and turned to walk away.

"I'm going to get it back, you know!" I exclaimed. "Demigod or not. No one's above the law."

Glo's scales flashed a mix of red and blue, a sign of her annoyance.

"Whatever you say, Detective," Jace replied with a casual wave over his shoulder.

* * *

"**A**re you sure you can get there on your own?" Sebastian asked as I stepped onto the boat. The small craft rocked beneath my feet.

The ferry between the islands ran every two hours, but I wanted to get to Splash Island immediately and not wait around for the next boat. That required finding a small dingy—which the former sheriff did for me in record time.

"Oh, sure," I said with more confidence than I felt.

I might not know my way around a boat, but water was my element. The ocean never steered me wrong. I wound the string around the top of the motor, gave a quick yank on the pull cord, and the engine roared to life. Sebastian hobbled over to untie the front rope while I saw to the one in the back.

"It's that way." Sebastian pointed to the north.

"Got it. Don't worry, I'll be fine."

With a nod, he stepped back onto the dock.

The salty breeze ruffled my hair as I steered the boat away from Neptune Oasis, the small waves lapping against the sides. The journey to Splash Island was a straightforward one, but according to the former sheriff, it would take about twenty minutes. Since I hadn't yet visited the island, I was curious to see how it differed from Neptune Oasis.

Even though it was still mid-morning, the sun was high in the sky, casting a brilliant path of light on the water. Everything seemed peaceful...the rhythmic hum of the engine lulling me into a sense of calm.

But just as the coastline of Neptune Oasis faded from view, the engine sputtered and died. The boat's momentum slowed, and I furrowed my brows in confusion. I leaned over and tried to restart the engine, but after several attempts, I collapsed in exhaustion.

"Come on!" I muttered, giving the pull cord one last yank.

Nothing.

"Great," I muttered. "Just what I need."

Bracing myself against the rocking boat, I inspected the engine, my mind racing to recall any bits of knowledge about boat engines I'd picked up over the years.

As I worked, the sea around me seemed to grow rougher, the waves cresting higher as they crashed against the boat. It was as if the ocean itself was determined to challenge my resolve, reminding me that even in my element, I wasn't invincible.

Without warning, a tentacle popped out of the water and plopped next to my foot.

"What the—" I broke off and laughed, dropping down to dip my hands into the water. I needed the connection with the liquid to hear my friend. "Hydra Ann? Is that you?"

"You caught me, Isla. Are you having problems?"

I'd first met Hydra Ann when I went to question her about the stolen gold coin and about her seeing Jace dive in the restricted area. We'd clicked immediately, and I made it a point to come out and swim with her as often as I could. I might live and work on land, but the minute my body hit the water and my tail fin appeared...it was like coming home.

Even though the sea was my life, I hadn't met many krakens in my time. My first glimpse of Hydra Ann had been daunting. Her tentacles had a span of nearly twenty-five feet. Shayla had also informed me Hydra Ann had a brother back on Enchanted Island who also policed the waters and watched for danger.

"Yes," I said. "The engine has stalled."

"I can pull you to wherever you are going."

"Splash Island. I need to question someone."

The tentacle inside the boat slowly retracted. *"Hold on, Isla."*

I stood and withdrew my hands from the water—breaking my contact with Hydra Ann. I sat back down on the wooden plank and thought about what Jace had said about overhearing Fredrick fighting with someone named Chester. Was Jace telling me the truth? Or was he just trying to divert my attention because he was guilty of murder?

❦ 4 ❧

Even though I'd spent four weeks in the Bermuda Triangle, I'd not yet made it to Splash Island. As I stepped from the boat and onto the small wooden dock, I tied off the boat and waved goodbye to Hydra Ann—promising I'd meet up for a midnight swim soon. I had no idea how I was going to get back to Neptune Oasis, but I had more pressing matters to worry about.

As I made my way up the sandy beach, I glanced around and took it all in. I noticed an immediate difference between Neptune Oasis and Splash Island. Neptune Oasis was more of a tourist destination, with beautiful cobblestone sidewalks, quaint buildings, amazing restaurants, and tons of shops. But here on Splash Island, there wasn't a single commercial building in sight. Instead, dozens of Tiki huts selling fruits and knickknacks were spread out as far as I could see, and lounge chairs with canopies also dotted the landscape.

The shoreline seemed to sparkle in the sunlight, as if every grain of sand was a tiny diamond. The lush green vegetation of palm trees and tropical flowers lined the coastline, providing a picturesque backdrop that only an enchanted island could.

The sound of waves crashing against the beach and birds crying overhead filled my ears as I strolled toward one of the nearby Tiki huts.

I stilled when someone cleared their throat. I glanced over at one of the canopy lounge chairs and groaned. Jace Solari was sprawled out on a chair…Glo perched at the bottom near his feet, flask in her claw.

"What are you doing here?" I demanded. "And how did you get here so fast?"

Jace chuckled. "I have my ways."

I scowled. "Wait. Did you see me needing help on the water?"

"It looked like you had everything under control." Jace sat up in the chair. "I envy you your connection with the sea life."

I rolled my eyes. "You're a demigod. I doubt you envy much."

He arched a perfectly groomed eyebrow. "Perhaps you don't know me as well as you think?"

"Let me repeat my earlier question," I said. "What are you doing here?"

"You need help, Fishy Witch," Glo said, her scales glowing purple and red. She took a healthy drink from her flask and grinned. "Anyone can see that."

I scowled. "I'm a PADA detective, thank you. I'm highly trained."

"Tell her," Glo demanded.

"Tell me what?" I mused.

"Let's see," Jace said. "Over the last three thousand or so years, I've been a healer, a doctor, an architect, an athlete in the first Greek Olympics, a monk, a—"

"Lie!" I cried. "No way have you ever been a monk!"

Jace threw back his head and laughed. "I didn't say a *celibate* monk. Anyway, I can also add herbalist, physician, explorer, and surgeon."

"That's a lot of medical history," I said.

"Descendant of Apollo," Jace said. "It's in my blood." He held up his hands. "Healing touch."

Glo cleared her throat and narrowed her beady little dragon eyes. "It's not just Greek god blood in you, dragon shifter! Remember that!"

Jace grinned and ran his hand down Glo's tiny back. "I don't forget, Glo. I also have dragon blood in me, Detective."

I gasped. "You can shift into a dragon? Why didn't I detect that?"

"As a demigod, I can conceal. Anyway, one reason I became a treasure hunter hundreds of years ago was because there's a part of me that's always yearning to discover something. I blame that on the dragon blood of my mother."

"That's right," Glo said, lifting her front claw in the air. "We do what we want…when we want!"

Jace high-fived Glo. "Always, my fiery little friend. It's the same reason I studied to be a PI—the desire to find answers."

I snorted. "You're a licensed PI? Seriously?"

Jace nodded. "I am." He held up one hand and grinned. "Honest."

I rolled my eyes. "The word 'honest' doesn't fit you."

"Maybe not, but I can still help you, Detective."

"You're a person of interest in this case," I said. "Don't forget that."

"So that's a no on the help?" Jace asked.

"That's a no on the help, Mr. Solari."

He held up a hand. "Your loss." He winked. "And call me Jace."

I sighed. "I want that gold coin, Mr. Solari."

I turned left and headed for the first Tiki hut I came to. The man working was kind enough to give me directions to Fredrick Longshore's law office, and ten minutes later, I was in the heart of downtown Splash Island.

Fredrick's law office was a quaint, two-story structure adorned with colorful shutters. A young woman in her mid-twenties sat on the steps leading to the entrance. Her shoulders trembled, and the faint sound of sniffles reached my ears. She looked up as I approached—her hazel eyes red and swollen from crying.

"Excuse me," I said. "Are you Celeste Zephyr?"

The blonde nodded as she wiped away a tear. "Yes, I am. Who are you?"

"I'm Detective Isla Ceartas. I'm the PADA detective for the Bermuda Triangle. I'm here to investigate the incident involving Fredrick Longshore."

At the mention of Fredrick's name, Celeste's face crumpled, and fresh tears spilled down her cheeks. She wiped them away hastily with the back of her hand. "I can't believe he's gone. I was here at the office when I got the first call from a client. They wanted to know if it was true!" Another tear fell and slowly slid down her cheek. "I just thought maybe he was late. Wednesdays are usually late nights for him, and sometimes he comes in late. He didn't have to be in court today, so I…" She trailed off and sighed. "He was a good man, despite what most people said about him."

I took a seat next to her on the steps, giving her a moment to compose herself. "I'm sorry for your loss, Celeste. Can you tell me about your relationship with Mr. Longshore?"

She took a shaky breath, her fingers twisting in her lap. "I haven't been his secretary long. Maybe a year and a half. He could be demanding, but he was fair, and he trusted me. We had a professional relationship, but he treated me like family."

"Did Mr. Longshore work here at the law office yesterday?"

"Yes."

"Do you know what time he left?"

"We both left around five, but Mr. Longshore had another appointment with a client on Neptune Oasis at seven."

I heard whistling down the street and glanced up to see Jace and Glo approach. I scowled...but Jace just ignored me and smiled at the weeping young girl.

"Oh," Celeste said, her hands flying to her chest. "Mr. Solari, I wasn't expecting you." Her eyes filled with tears. "I'm afraid I have awful news, Mr. Solari. Mr. Longshore has been murdered!"

"That's awful, indeed. I'm sorry for your loss," Jace said. "How are you holding up?"

"Not good." The shy sea witch brushed a tear off her cheek. "But thanks for asking, Mr. Solari."

"Why are you here?" I demanded, cutting off the pleasantries.

"I came to see my attorney," Jace lied smoothly.

"That's what law-abiding citizens do," Glo added.

I shifted to block the two from my view and continued to question Celeste.

"Who was the client?" I asked Celeste between clenched teeth.

Celeste's brows furrowed. "What?"

I sighed and softened my tone. It wasn't Celeste's fault Jace made me crazy. "Who was Fredrick Longshore meeting last night around seven on Neptune Oasis?"

Celeste bit her lip. "I'm not sure I should say."

"Celeste," I said, "this is a murder investigation. You need to answer my questions."

"I'm sure Ms. Zephyr will be happy to cooperate," Jace said. "Won't you, Celeste?"

"Oh, of course!" She smiled hesitantly at Jace. "It's like Mr. Solari said. I'd like to help."

Jace winked at the flustered secretary. "You can call me Jace."

It was all I could do not to roll my eyes.

Celeste looked dreamily at Jace, and I swear I could practically see the younger sea witch planning their wedding.

I cleared my throat, interrupting their moment. "Celeste?"

"What?" Celeste blinked.

"Who was Fredrick Longshore meeting last night?" I repeated slowly.

"Oh, right. He had a meeting with Donald Warner at the Bermuda Bistro at seven."

"What can you tell me about Donald?" I asked.

Celeste pressed her lips together. "I hope it's okay to say, but I don't particularly care for him. He's constantly in here because his ex-wife drags him back to court since he never pays his child support, things like that. She's *constantly* calling here to complain about Donald not paying." She shrugged. "I don't know what last night's meeting was about. Mr. Longshore didn't tell me specifics. But he did text me around eight to let me know he finished his meeting and how much time to bill Donald Warner for. I know Mr. Longshore and Donald were friendly. Like I got the feeling they'd known each other a long time."

"And after his meeting with Donald Warner?" I mused.

"After that," Celeste said, "Fredrick was meeting a group of guys for their weekly Whiskey Wednesday at Barnacle Bar & Grill. That's all I know."

I glanced at Jace out of the corner of my eye, remembering his lead from earlier. "Who's Chester, Celeste? I've been told Fredrick may have had an argument with someone named Chester recently."

Celeste cleared her throat. "Oh, that's probably Chester Montross. He's a lionfish shifter over on Neptune Oasis." Celeste shivered. "He blames Mr. Longshore for doing jail time." She snorted. "I mean, he had the stolen items on him when he was arrested! What did he expect? And if Mr. Longshore couldn't get his charges reduced or dismissed, then you know the man was guilty! Anyway, Chester's been calling and harassing Mr. Longshore." She sniffed and wiped her nose. "I guess maybe he could have hurt Mr. Longshore."

"Anyone else you can think of who might have wanted to hurt your former boss?" I asked.

Celeste shrugged. "I dunno. Maybe you should talk to his ex-wife or his current girlfriend. They might be able to help you more." She sucked in a ragged breath, her eyes wide. "Oh, maybe Sam Stringer?"

"Who is Sam Stringer?" I asked.

"He's a lionfish shifter on Neptune Oasis. He blames Mr. Longshore for his daughter's accident." Celeste held up a hand and looked imploringly at Jace. "Not that it's true, of course."

"Why does he blame Mr. Longshore?" I asked.

"Well, this happened about four months before I was hired on," Celeste said. "I think it's been almost two years now that the accident happened. From what I understand, a drunk driver hit Sam Stringer's daughter when she and her mom were crossing the street on Neptune Oasis. The daughter was seriously injured, but because they'd been jaywalking, Mr. Longshore could fight it." She held up her hands. "Again, I wasn't working here at the time, so I might not have it right. You should ask Mr. Stringer.

But Mr. Longshore did tell me that Sam Stringer cornered him outside the courthouse after the verdict was handed down, and he threatened to kill Mr. Longshore." She sighed. "Then, about five months ago, Sam Stringer was arrested for hitting Mr. Longshore in the nose."

"Really?" I mused. "Okay. Anyone else who might have wanted to do harm to Mr. Longshore?"

"I don't think so."

"What's Fredrick's ex-wife's name?" I asked.

"Wren Sellars," Celeste said. "They divorced earlier this year." She smiled sheepishly. "They didn't have an amicable divorce. It was pretty public and brutal."

I nodded. "Okay. You said you left the office around five yesterday. Where did you go?"

"Home to my apartment on Neptune Oasis. Well, I stopped by the deli down the street from my apartment and picked up a tuna fish sandwich and chips, and then I went home." She glanced around me to stare at Jace. "I usually cook, but last night I was too tired. Besides, my favorite show was on last night."

"And what show is that?" Jace asked.

"Dancing with the Supernatural Stars."

"Who's your favorite?" Glo asked, her scales glowing pink and orange. "I like Sasha Waterfall."

"He's good," Celeste agreed. "But my favorite is Collin Atwell."

"Let's bring it back," I said, trying not to show my frustration. "What time did the show end?"

"Eight."

"Then what did you do?" I asked.

"I had a glass of wine and read for a while, and then I went to bed."

I nodded. "Anyone living at your house who can corroborate that?"

Celeste's mouth dropped. "Are you implying I might have killed my boss?" She slapped her hands over her chest. "Not only did I like Mr. Longshore, but I love this job." She sniffed and swiped at a tear. "I have no idea what I'll do now." She looked at Jace. "I guess I'll have to find a new job."

He sat down on the other side of her. "I'm sure you'll have no problem finding new employment, Celeste."

Celeste smiled, and she batted her long lashes at him. "You think so?"

"I know so," Jace assured her.

"We about done here?" Glo asked. "I could use some food."

I narrowed my eyes at the dragon. "You are free to leave any time you want. In fact, I'll insist again you both do."

Jace grinned. "So noted, Detective."

When he didn't make a move to leave, I turned back to Celeste. "Is there anyone who can corroborate where you were last night?"

She shook her head, her blonde curls flying around her head. "No." She gave Jace a sly smile. "I live alone." She lifted her left hand. "No ring."

I sighed. "We're done here. Before I leave, Celeste, I'll want the contact information for Donald Warner, Chester Montross, Wren Sellars, and Sam Stringer."

Celeste bit her lip. "Well, I guess. If you're sure I won't get in trouble."

I arched an eyebrow. "Mr. Longshore is dead. I don't think he's going to be mad that you gave me information that might help capture his killer."

Tears filled the pretty girl's eyes. "You don't have to keep reminding me he's dead."

Glo snickered, her scales glowing green and blue. "Yeah. Have a heart, Detective."

I gave her a hard look before turning my attention back to Celeste. "Let's go inside so we can get the contact information I need. Oh, and I'm going to need Mr. Longshore's address. I want to stop by his place and make sure his house is locked up."

5

After gathering the necessary information from Celeste, I parted ways with Jace and Glo and walked the two miles to Fredrick's house. It was a beautiful two-story limestone home with a circle drive up front and a swimming pool around back. Everything was locked up nice and tight, so I decided to return later if I needed to look around inside. Doc Bowers had probably run across Fredrick's keys by now and placed them into evidence. With no sign of a forced entry or anything out of place, it didn't look like the killer had returned to Fredrick's house to look for anything.

I walked back to where I'd docked my boat and was about to jump in the water and just swim back to Neptune Oasis—thank you mermaid genes—when Jace sidled up next to me...Glo glowering on his shoulder.

"Seriously?" I mused. "What do I have to do to get rid of you two?"

Jace grinned. "Now, why would you want rid of me, Detective? I simply came by to see if you'd like a ride home."

"On your back? No thanks. Part mermaid. I can simply swim back to Neptune Oasis."

"I actually fixed your boat while you were gone."

That brought me up short. "Oh. Well, thank you."

"You're welcome. Can Glo and I hitch a ride back with you?"

"Why not fly back? You are a dragon shifter, after all."

"Yeah," Glo said. "We can just fly back."

"I'm a little tired," Jace said. "I thought maybe you'd take pity on an old demigod."

I knew he was playing me, but I couldn't very well say no after he went to all the trouble of fixing my boat.

"Let's go."

We made it back to Neptune Oasis without incident, and after a lot of threats on my part, the two finally agreed to drop me off on the north side where I'd left my Polaris earlier that morning, and then drive the boat back to the dock where Sebastian had borrowed it from.

My first stop was the Barnacle Bar & Grill, a rustic establishment perched near the shoreline, just off the beaten path from the hustle and bustle of town. The interior was cozy and filled with the hum of conversation and the clinking of glasses. I headed for the bar, where a woman with aquamarine hair was busy wiping down the counter.

"Excuse me," I said. "I'm wondering if you can help me? Were you by chance working last night?"

The woman turned her gaze toward me, her eyes a striking shade of turquoise. Her name tag read Nymphadora. "I was. What can I do for you?"

"I'm Detective Isla Ceartas," I said. "I'm investigating the death of Fredrick Longshore. I heard he was a regular here on Wednesday nights."

Nymphadora's lips dipped into a frown. "I heard about that. I thought about giving the sheriff a call until I remembered he retired."

"I'm the new PADA detective for the Bermuda Triangle. What did you want to tell the sheriff?"

Nymphadora leaned in closer. "Fredrick and his buddies are usually a lively bunch. They come in on Wednesdays at least two or three times a month. They drink whiskey and stay until around eleven and then head home. But last night, Fredrick wasn't himself. He seemed agitated."

"How so?"

"First, he had a shoving match with Chester Montross."

"Chester Montross?" No way was there two Chester Montrosses on the island. That meant the guy who'd been calling and threatening Fredrick was at the same bar last night. "So the two men had a fight?"

"Not really a fight," Nymphadora said. "More like a shove-and-shout kind of thing. I broke them up and told them to either take it outside or go back to their tables." She smiled. "They went back to their tables."

"Did the two men speak the rest of the night?"

Nymphadora shook her head. "Not that I know of. Next time I paid attention to what was going on was when Fredrick was yelling into his cell phone. I didn't catch everything, but I got the impression whoever was on the other end wanted to meet up. Fredrick kept demanding to know who was speaking—ya know, like he didn't recognize the number or voice. Finally, Fredrick gets good and mad and says he'll be there in thirty minutes."

"But he never said where, specifically?" I mused.

"Nope. Not that I heard."

"And he never said a name?"

"Again, nope."

I nodded, processing the information. "One last question."

"What's that?"

"Could you check to see if you have Fredrick's receipt from last night? I'm looking for what time he paid his tab."

"Sure. It'll take me a second to print it off. Hang on a minute."

"Oh, and what about Chester Montross? Can you see what time he paid for his tab as well?"

Nymphadora nodded and headed down a hallway next to the bar. She returned a few minutes later with two slips of paper in her hand and handed them to me. I quickly scanned the receipts.

"Looks like Fredrick Longshore paid at 9:42," I said. "And Chester Montross paid for his drinks at 9:27."

"I'd say that sounds right," Nymphadora said.

"Thanks. You've been a great help."

As I hopped in the driver's side of the Polaris, I thought about the timeline. It had taken me thirty-five minutes to drive from where Fredrick's body had been found to the Barnacle Bar & Grill. So if he told the person on the phone he'd see them in thirty minutes, then assuming he left straight from the bar and drove to the north side of Neptune Oasis, that would put his time of death between ten-fifteen and seven this morning.

It was almost twelve-thirty when I parked in front of the Bermuda Triangle PADA Station. Nana was sitting at her desk eating a to-go box of tea sandwiches–crusts cut off— and chips from Kyra's bakery.

"Got you one, too," she said as I dropped down in a chair across from her desk.

"Thanks, Nana. It's already been a long day."

I spent the next few minutes filling her in on the crime scene, my trip out to Splash Island to question Celeste Zephyr—minus my run-in with Jace—and about the conversation I had with the server at Barnacle Bar & Grill.

"Sounds like you already got a lot of suspects," Nana said, taking a huge bite of her sandwich. "PADA can do all the background for me."

"I'd like you to run Chester Montross. He evidently didn't appreciate the fact Fredrick couldn't get him off all his charges like he had other criminals, and they had an altercation at the bar last night. Then there's Wren Sellars. I don't know much except for what the secretary said. And that's that Wren and Fredrick didn't divorce on amicable terms."

"I assume you want me to run Celeste Zephyr?" Nana mused. "From how you described her hero worship of Fredrick, maybe they were more than just employee and employer."

I crinkled my nose. "Eww. She's like twenty-five, and he had to be at least in his late fifties. But I guess you never know? So, yes, run Celeste Zephyr. Also run Sam Stringer and his wife. I didn't catch her name—sorry about that—but the story Celeste told was that Sam's daughter was in a serious accident, and Fredrick got the person who ran her over off on a technicality. I'll definitely want to find out more there." I paused and took a bite of my sandwich, thinking about my next request. "I'd also like you to see what PADA can give you with regards to Jace Solari. I'd like to know what they say about the rogue demigod."

Nana looked up from her notepad. "You really think he's a viable suspect? That he murdered Fredrick?"

I scowled and thought about the handsome, arrogant demigod. "I don't know. I can't get a read on him and that dragon he has." I set my sandwich on the plate. "Oh, hey! Get this. He's not only a demigod, but he's also a dragon shifter! Can you believe that?"

"A dragon shifter *and* a demigod," Nana mused. "Doesn't seem fair."

"And he tried to tell me he was a licensed PI and could help me solve this case."

Nana's eyebrow raised. "Did he now? Did you take the handsome devil up on his offer?"

I narrowed my eyes at Nana. "No, I did not. And don't you, either!"

"A little excitement might do you good, Isla," Nana said.

I stood and grabbed a madeleine out of the bakery box. "I gotta go. I want to talk to as many suspects as I can today."

Nana cackled. "Don't think I don't know what turning tail and running looks like, girl! It hasn't been that long since your grandfather was alive!"

"Nana! Shame on you."

"I'm only ninety-five. I still got plenty of good years ahead of me."

I rolled my eyes and headed for the door. "And stop drinking on the job! I can smell the rum on your breath."

6

After leaving Nana at the station, I headed toward Ocean Oasis Spa to talk with Wren Sellars, Fredrick's ex-wife. The spa was on the east side of town, so it took about ten minutes to reach in the Polaris. The main building was a sprawling villa made of moonlit marble, with graceful arches and delicate spires.

As I parked in front of the curved driveway, I couldn't help but wonder how the staff would react to seeing a vehicle marked with the new Bermuda Triangle PADA logo plastered on the side.

"Good afternoon," a perky girl of about twenty-two said as I stepped out of the Polaris.

"Good afternoon," I said. "This is an official visit. Can I leave my vehicle here? I won't be long."

The girl, a cuttlefish shifter, smiled and nodded, her blonde hair changing to a beautiful purple hue. "Of course."

I stepped onto a stone pathway that sparkled and glittered, and every step I took changed the colors of the stones. The wooden archway beckoned me forward, and I hurried past the lush garden lining the walkway. In the distance, I could see multiple wooden bridges that crossed a stream of water.

I turned to the girl now working by the flowers. "Why are there so many bridges for one stream of water?"

"When you cross a bridge, it whispers words of encouragement to take with you on your walk."

"That's amazing," I said. "I'll have to try it out sometime."

I opened the spa's wooden door and strode inside. I hurried toward the counter, trying not to gape at the cascading crystal stalactites that dropped from the ceiling with their soft luminescent glow of purples, blues, and silvers. I couldn't help but smile at the enchanted mural on the wall that depicted a group of beautiful mermaids beckoning customers forward.

"What is that amazing smell?" I asked the selkie shifter behind the counter. "It's wonderful."

And it really was. It was like a combination of exotic flowers, herbs, and something else I couldn't put my finger on.

The woman smiled. "Spa secret. I'm Shelby Stewart, the spa's manager. How may I help you..." She glanced down at my uniform. "Sheriff?"

"Detective," I said. "I'm the new PADA detective for the island now that Sheriff Sebastian has retired."

"Of course. What can I do for you, Detective? Were you needing a spa treatment? We specialize in seaweed wraps, but we also offer mystical mud baths to help rejuvenate both your body and soul. Or maybe you're in need of a massage? We have gifted masseurs on staff."

I remembered my friend Shayla Stone-Loci telling me about the couples' massage they had on their honeymoon and how her husband, Alex, had gotten a massage from an octopus shifter. Totally freaked him out at first to feel eight tentacles on him at once.

"Not today," I said. "I'm actually looking for the owner. Wren Sellars? Is she here this morning?"

Shelby Stewart shook her head. "I'm afraid not. She called about an hour ago and told me she wasn't feeling well and wouldn't be in." She frowned. "Is everything okay? Is Wren okay?"

"Yes," I said. "I just needed a word with her. I thought I'd stop by here first. I can drive to her house."

"Do you know where she lives? I mean, I feel like I shouldn't just hand out that information."

I didn't tell her PADA linked me with a program that mapped every citizen and business on the three islands thanks to an IT forensics guy from Enchanted Island. The program was a game-changer for many PADA agents.

"I know where she lives," I said. "I'll try her at home."

"Okay, if you're sure. I hope Wren is okay." She smiled sheepishly. "Also, I wouldn't be doing my job if I didn't invite you back when you're off duty to partake of our services."

I glanced around the magical, relaxing room. "Oh, I'm sure I'll be back. Thank you."

I headed back out to my Polaris, waving to the young cuttle-fish shifter who was now pulling weeds. Hopping behind the wheel, I pulled up Wren Sellars' address and followed the route set out for me.

It wasn't long before I pulled into the driveway of a modest but rundown house where Wren Sellars was living—a stark contrast to the luxurious aura of the Ocean Oasis Spa that Wren owned, and the home on Splash Island I assumed she lived in when she was married to Fredrick. Stepping out of my vehicle, I made my way up the cracked walkway and knocked on the front door. Moments later, the door opened, revealing a woman with shoulder-length auburn hair, green eyes, and an air of sophistication.

"Good afternoon," I said. "I'm Detective Isla Ceartas."

"I know why you're here, Detective," the mermaid said. "I received a phone call about two hours ago telling me my ex-husband had been murdered."

"So you know I'm investigating the death of Fredrick Longshore? May I speak with you for a moment?"

Wren regarded me with a mixture of suspicion and wariness. "Of course. Please come in." She gestured for me to enter, and I stepped into a small living room that had clearly seen better days. The two cream-colored couches were threadbare, some with torn cushions and others sporting numerous stains. A cream and teal milk-painted coffee table sat between the couches...candles and stones scattered across the top. Wren had artfully draped muslin cloths with bejeweled edges over the two floor lamps. I'd seen the look in upscale magazines before, and even though Wren had tried to give the room a shabby-chic look, it fell short.

"Thank you for your time, Wren," I said as I took a seat on a well-worn couch. "I understand you were once married to Fredrick Longshore?"

Wren nodded, her expression neutral. "Yes, that's correct. We divorced earlier this year."

"I'm sorry to bring up painful memories, but I'm hoping you can provide some insight into his life," I continued. "I understand you own the Ocean Oasis Spa?"

Wren's gaze locked with mine for a moment, her eyes narrowing slightly. "Yes, that's my business. Why do you ask?"

"Do you specialize in seaweed wraps?"

"We specialize in many things, but seaweed wraps are a service we offer. Why?"

"Fredrick Longshore was found murdered with enchanted

seaweed," I said. "I'm trying to gather any information that might help us understand why he was targeted."

Wren's lips tightened, and she visibly tensed. "Enchanted seaweed? That's... disturbing."

I nodded, noting her reaction. "It is."

Wren snorted and sat back on the couch. "This island is filled with magicals. There are sea witches, mermaids, selkies, lionfish, and tons more supernaturals who can wield water magic. Not just mermaids and sea witches."

"I'm aware. I also picked up on mermaid magic in the enchanted net he was encased in."

Wren sucked in a breath. "I hadn't heard about how he was found. Just that he was murdered."

"I'd like to know more about your relationship with Fredrick. Did anything significant happen between you two during the divorce?"

A shadow crossed Wren's features, and she sighed. "Our divorce was...messy. Being an attorney, Fredrick knew the ins and outs of the law. In the end, he got the house and a whole lot more. I barely kept my business, the Ocean Oasis Spa." Wren's jaw tightened, and I saw the pain in her eyes. "Fredrick Long-shore screwed me over, Detective. The spa has been my lifeline, and I've had to work extra hard to keep it up and running."

"And how has that been going for you?" I asked, my tone gentle.

Wren's voice took on a bitter edge. "I'm barely making ends meet. That house he got in the divorce? It's a beautiful beach-front property with a pool in the back." She gestured around the room. "Meanwhile, I'm living here."

"I'm sorry to hear that," I said sincerely. "The divorce seems to have left you in a difficult position."

"Of course it has," Wren snapped, her anger simmering

beneath the surface. "Fredrick never cared how his actions hurt me or caused me to struggle. I think he got enjoyment out of it." She glanced at the wall. "Fredrick only cared about himself."

I observed her for a moment, sensing the depth of her emotions. "As a mermaid, you can wield magic?"

"I can." She met my eyes. "I also come from a long line of sea witches."

"Where were you last night between the hours of ten and seven this morning?"

"I figured you'd ask, eventually. The spa closes at eight every night. I'm open seven days a week, but the hours I put in are flexible. I was at the spa last night when it closed. I met up with some girlfriends at the Sunken Vines Winery afterward for Wine Wednesdays. We had drinks and socialized until around ten o'clock. After that, I came home and went to bed."

"And you live alone?"

"That's right." Tears filled her pretty green eyes. "I loved Fredrick Longshore once, you know. Despite everything he's done to me, I would never murder him."

"Do you know of anyone who might want to hurt him?"

Wren snorted. "Plenty. When we were married, we were always getting phone calls and threats. I remember once going to our car after dining out, and someone had stuck a note under the windshield wiper promising to hurt him."

"But no one comes to mind right now?"

"We haven't been close for a while now. If he's pissed someone off recently, I don't know about it."

I stood and handed her my business card. "I appreciate your cooperation. If you think of anything else that might be relevant, please don't hesitate to contact me."

7

After leaving Wren's house, I headed to interview the current girlfriend, Missy Weiss. Figuring she'd heard the news by now, I elected to go to her home first. After knocking on the door for a few minutes, I gave up and headed to her shop, Pendants & Pearls, a charming jewelry store across the street and down two buildings from the bakery. I'd walked past the store many times since my move to the island, but I'd never gone in.

That was about to change.

The store was small and quaint, with soft pink-painted walls and natural hardwood floors. Glass cases displayed a glittering array of beach-themed jewelry, including sparkling shell pendants, starfish brooches, and lustrous strands of pearls. The scent of vanilla and coconut mingled with the soft instrumental music playing in the background, creating a sense of understated elegance.

A woman with dark hair and red, swollen eyes greeted me when I walked in. While the island didn't consist only of water shifters and sea witches, it made up the majority. That wasn't the case for Missy Weiss. As I lifted my hand in greeting to the vampire, she quickly wiped her tears away and slipped on a false smile.

"Good afternoon," I said. "I'm Detective Isla Ceartas, and I'm looking for Missy Weiss."

"That's me," the woman confirmed, taking a deep breath. "I thought you might stop by. Celeste Zephyr, Fredrick's secretary, called me a couple hours ago." A tear trickled down her cheek. "I just can't believe this has happened. We're both just devastated."

"How is she holding up?" I asked as I approached the counter. "She was pretty upset when I spoke to her early this morning."

"She can't believe Fredrick is gone, either. It's... just so surreal."

"I'm sorry for your loss. You were Fredrick's current girlfriend?"

Missy's eyes softened with a mixture of sadness and fondness. "We've been dating for about five months."

I arched an eyebrow. "Five months?"

"I know what you're thinking," the vampire said with a hint of defense. "He'd just gotten divorced from his first wife, but that had nothing to do with me. Or our relationship. I started dating Fredrick after his divorce."

I nodded. "Okay. And when was the last time you talked to him?"

"Yesterday afternoon, around four. I told him I'd catch up with him today." She smiled and wiped at another tear. "A couple times a month on Wednesdays, he'd meet up with a couple of his guy friends, and they'd hang out at a bar and drink. It was important to him, and so I respected that time."

"What about you? What did you do last night?"

"I almost always meet my aunt for dinner on those Wednesdays. Last night was no exception." Missy's expression turned thoughtful. "I was home by eight, and then I jumped on Broom Chat with my sister, who lives in Charmed Falls. We talked until around nine, and then I went to bed."

"And you didn't hear from Fredrick at all?"

"Not once," Missy admitted.

"Do you know of anyone who might want to hurt Fredrick?"

"I've been thinking about that since I heard the news. A couple people come to mind. He'd been talking a lot about Chester Montross and Sam Stringer. Those names came up frequently. I never pressed him about it. I figured he'd share if he wanted."

"And he didn't share with you?"

She shrugged. "Not really. I mean, I know why each man would hate him, but I don't know specifics why lately they've been hounding him."

"The group of men he usually has drinks with on Wednesdays. Can you give me a name or two?"

Missy gazed thoughtfully up at the ceiling. "Let's see. I'd say probably you should talk with Barry Amos. He and Fredrick were pretty close. The other two guys were really just acquaintances."

"Where can I find Barry? Do you know?"

"I assume at the bank around the corner, Neptune Oasis Savings & Loan. He's a branch manager."

"Thank you." I handed her my card. "If you remember anything that might be relevant, please don't hesitate to contact me."

Missy nodded. "Of course, Detective. I know Fredrick had a bit of a reputation, but he wasn't like that with me. He was a good man. He didn't deserve this."

"I understand."

"Find out who did this to him, will you? I want to make sure they pay."

"I intend to."

* * *

Barry Amos was indeed at Neptune Oasis Savings & Loan. He was just finishing a meeting when I asked to see him. The secretary must have told him who I was beforehand because when he hurried over to shake my hand, it was a little too enthusiastic and just a little too insincere.

"Hello, Detective Ceartas. I'm Barry Amos, the branch manager here at the bank." He pumped my hand vigorously five or six times, and with each pump, a lock of hair fell against his forehead. "Lovely to meet you." He finally let go of my hand and lifted one of his in the air. "I know this is about an unfortunate incident, but I want you to know if you're looking to buy a home here in the Bermuda Triangle, we'd be happy to supply you a loan. Working for PADA, I'm sure you'd have no problem qualifying."

I barely refrained from wiping my palm on my pants. "Thank you, Mr. Amos, but that's not why I'm here."

"Oh, I know. I know. I've heard the horrible news." He gestured me inside an office encased entirely of glass. "Step inside, please. We can have more privacy...away from prying eyes and ears."

Was he joking? Everyone in the bank could still see me in the glass office. "Thank you." I stepped inside the office and scrunched my nose. Barry had eaten something ghastly for lunch, and the smell still permeated the air.

"Sit. Sit." He indicated a chair in front of his desk as he hurried around to sit on the other side. Steepling his fingers

49

together, he leaned over the desk. "Now, what did you need to know about Fredrick?"

"You were friends?"

"Since high school."

"You were with him last night?"

Barry nodded and leaned back in his seat. "Yes. We met up a little after eight at Barnacle Bar & Grill—something we often do on Wednesday nights. Blow off a little steam. You understand?"

"Of course. And Fredrick was there last night?"

"Yes."

"Were you still at the bar when Fredrick left around nine-forty?"

Barry nodded. "I was." He flashed me a grin. "I was chatting up this charming mermaid tourist. Lovely woman."

"I see. Getting back to Fredrick, how did he seem to you? How was his demeanor around the time he was getting ready to leave?"

Barry glanced at the ceiling as if deep in thought. "I've been thinking about last night ever since I heard the news. And I guess I can say he seemed upset when he told me he was leaving." He looked at me and shrugged sheepishly. "I know I probably should have taken more interest, but I was into the mermaid."

"Of course."

"Anyway, he just told me he had to leave." He snapped his fingers. "Oh, I asked if he was okay. I mean, I knew he'd gotten into a shoving match with Chester Montross a little earlier in the bar. So I thought maybe that was why he was upset. When I asked if he was okay, he just said he had something important to take care of." He shrugged. "Like I said, he was upset and even a little angry...but that was Fredrick. He was always like that." He grinned. "Downfalls of being an alpha barracuda."

I groaned inwardly. This guy was seriously too much. "Did Fredrick ever talk to you about someone threatening him?"

Barry lifted one hand in the air. "Again, pitfalls of being a defense attorney. Everyone pretty much hated him...until they needed him." He wrapped his knuckles on the desk. "I'm sorry I can't be of more help, Detective Ceartas, but I have another meeting scheduled that I need to keep. Will we be much longer?"

"No, I think that's all the questions I have for now." If this guy was Fredrick's closest friend, I'd hate to see how broken up the other two guys in their little boys' club had been when they heard about Fredrick's murder. They probably didn't even bat an eye at the announcement. "Here's my card. Call me if you think of anything else."

I saw the gleam in Barry's eyes when he glanced at my card.

"And, Barry," I said. "Only call me if you have something to tell me about Fredrick. Understand?"

Barry stood and pocketed my card. "Oh, of course, Detective. Of course. Wouldn't dream of calling for any other reason." He winked at me. "Unless, of course, you want me to?"

"Have a good day, Mr. Amos."

8

My next stop was to talk with Chester Montross. The drive took me to a neighborhood that was far less polished than even where Wren Sellars now lived. The house was bare, the paint peeling from its clapboard siding, and the front porch sagged with age. Weeds tangled in the path to the door, and not a single window had a light shining through. I stepped out of the Polaris and approached the front door.

As I knocked on the door, it swung open to reveal a middle-aged man with a weathered face and tired eyes. His disheveled appearance and the atmosphere of the home told its own story.

"Mr. Montross?" I mused.

"Yeah, that's me," he grunted, his voice tinged with irritation.

"Isla Ceartas. I'm a detective with PADA, currently taking over law enforcement on the Bermuda Triangle. I'd like to ask you a few questions about Fredrick Longshore."

Chester Montross grunted. "Yeah? You and everyone else." He stepped back from the door and gestured me inside. "Might as well come in, and we'll make this a party."

I followed him into the house. The smell of bacon grease and filth lingered in the air. The living room was cluttered, and the overall atmosphere was stale and tense.

"Well hello, Detective," Jace Solari said from the couch. "Isn't this a surprise?"

I scowled at the infuriating man, and then turned my attention to Glo. I had to bite back a smile. It was obvious she was displeased to see me.

"You want something to drink?" Chester asked, motioning toward a half-empty bottle of cheap whiskey.

"No, thank you," I declined politely. "I'm here to ask you about your recent interactions with Fredrick Longshore."

Chester's eyes flared with a mix of anger and resentment. "Yeah, I had interactions with him, all right."

I held up my hand to stop him from talking and turned to Jace. "Mr. Solaris, I'm going to insist you leave. This is a police matter, and you are not law enforcement."

Chester Montross snorted. "Isn't that just like the cops? Always demanding something from you."

Jace smiled and stood up from the couch, smoothing down his black t-shirt. "Of course, Detective Ceartas. I meant no disrespect. I just stopped by to commiserate with my new friend, Chester. Seems we both disliked Fredrick Longshore."

Glo gave me one more baleful glare before zipping ahead of Jace, her scales glowing red and black. "We don't want to share with you anyway, Fishy Witch."

I rolled my eyes at Jace. "Be sure to shut the door behind you."

Jace winked at me. "Of course, Detective."

The minute the door closed, I turned to Chester Montross. "You knew Fredrick Longshore?"

"Oh, I knew the lying barracuda." Chester's fingers clenched into fists, and the bitterness in his voice was palpable. "He promised me I wouldn't do a single day of time. Said he had connections. Said he could get me off. I believed him. And then I spent six months in that hellhole on the mainland."

"Jail?" I asked, my voice neutral.

"Yeah, jail." Chester spat out the word as if it was a curse. "I lost my job because of him." He leaned down and picked up the bottle on the coffee table. He didn't bother with a glass...just tipped it to his lips and swallowed. "And now no one will hire me."

I didn't think it was wise to tell him he actually lost his job because he was caught with stolen goods in his possession.

"My wife's working two full-time jobs just to make ends meet while I'm stuck here with nothing."

I nodded. "I'm sure that's difficult."

"You're darn right it's difficult."

"You were at the Barnacle Bar & Grill last night?" I asked.

"Yeah."

"I have a witness who says she saw the two of you fighting. Can you tell me what the fight was about?"

Chester's eyes darkened, and his voice grew more heated. "We fought about how he screwed me over, how he lied, and how I ended up paying the price. He thought he could just walk away from that, but he was wrong."

Was this guy seriously unaware of how badly he was digging himself into a hole?

"What time did you leave the bar?" I asked.

I already knew the answer, but I wanted to see if Chester would tell the truth.

Chester shrugged. "I dunno. Maybe nine or nine-thirty. I was there to watch the game on the TV. So it probably ended around that time."

"Where did you go after you left the bar?"

Chester's eyes narrowed, his anger simmering beneath the surface. "I went home."

"What time did you get in?" I asked.

Chester shrugged. "Dunno. Maybe around 9:45. Don't take long to get home from the Barnacle."

"Was your wife home?"

"No. Last night she had the graveyard shift at the old folks' home. Goes in at nine and gets off around six."

"Is she here?" I asked. "I'd like to speak with her."

"She ain't here. She's at a different job today."

"She's back at work again this afternoon?" I asked, trying not to sound shocked.

Chester scowled. "We gotta have money, and she don't mind. Besides, she didn't have to go in until eleven. She rested for a couple hours. She's a workhorse, my Sally."

I grunted noncommittally. "Did you see Fredrick Longshore leave the Barnacle shortly after you left? Maybe see him in the parking lot?"

"No."

I knew Chester left the Barnacle Bar & Grill around nine-thirty, and Fredrick received a phone call that left him upset and leaving the bar around nine-forty. A little too coincidental for me. That gave Chester both means and motive, but I didn't want to jump to conclusions.

"So you came straight home from the bar and stayed here all night and morning? Never left?"

"That's what I just said."

I handed him my card. "If you remember anything else, or if you think of anything that might be relevant to the investigation, please don't hesitate to reach out."

"Yeah, right. I'll be sure to do that."

9

Stepping outside Chester's house, I found Jace casually leaning against my Polaris…Glo perched on his shoulder, flask in hand.

"I might have some information for you," Jace said, a hint of teasing in his voice.

"Is it about the gold coin?" I retorted. "Because that's all I want from you, Jace Solari."

"Don't be like that, Detective." He pushed off the Polaris, and Glo flew from his shoulder, hovering between us. "I think you know I didn't have anything to do with Fredrick Longshore's death. I was sitting right next to you when Celeste Zephyr gave you much better suspects. I still think we should work together."

Annoyance sparked within me. I tried to push past him. "Not interested, Demigod."

"Just leave her be, Jace," Glo snapped. "I don't get why you're so invested in helping the Fishy Witch, anyway. We can figure this out on our own. We don't need her."

I glanced at Glo, her bioluminescent scales shifting between shades of purple and green. It dawned on me that beneath her snark and attitude, she was actually feeling something I hadn't expected—jealousy. Glo was jealous of me.

"Whaddya got?" I asked, my curiosity piqued.

Jace grinned. "I thought you'd never ask. Before stopping by here, I visited the Barnacle Bar & Grill. I spoke to the bartender, and–"

"I already did that," I said. "I know what you know. But thanks, anyway."

Jace cleared his throat. "Can I finish, Detective?"

I rolled my eyes. "Fine. Finish."

He grinned, and I tried not to stare at the dimple that appeared in his cheek. "Anyway, I spoke to the bartender, and she told me about Fredrick *and* Chester Montross both being at the bar. She told me about their altercation, of both men leaving, and at what time. As I was exiting the bar, this nice waitress stopped me and told me something else. Something new."

I arched an eyebrow and crossed my arms over my chest. "Nice waitress?"

Glo snorted, her scales shimmering a pale green. "She was hot for the demigod."

I grinned. "That I believe. So what did this overly helpful server tell you?"

"Well, it seems my new friend remembers Chester Montross because he didn't tip her. A huge no-no. So she's already angry about that, and then she tells me she almost runs him over in town later that night. Intrigued by this, I asked her more questions. She tells me she closed down the bar, which meant she left the bar around one in the morning. As she was driving home, Chester Montross was out wandering the streets. He crossed the street in front of her mini cooper, and she almost hit him."

"She's sure it was him? Chester Montross?" I demanded.

Jace nodded. "Yep. He hit her hood with his hand. Yelled at her. Then took off in the opposite direction."

I glanced at the Montross house. Chester Montross had just told me he came straight home from the bar and stayed in the rest of the night and morning. Never leaving his house. So either this server was mistaken about who she'd seen, or Chester Montross had just lied to me.

"And this was around one in the morning?" I confirmed.

"That's what she told me," Jace said.

"Us," Glo said. "She told *us*."

Jace smiled. "So now you want in, Glo?"

Glo glared at me before flying to land on Jace's shoulder. "I want in. You and me, Jace. Just like the old days. We solve this case, and then we get off this dumb island."

"I guess that was your free tip," Jace said. "Glo says no more fraternizing with the enemy. We'll solve this on our own."

I lifted my finger and pointed it at him. "Jace Solari, you are *not* a PADA detective. You have no jurisdiction in this case. In fact, *you're* a suspect. So don't try to–"

"C'mon, partner," Glo said, interrupting my tirade. "Let's go question our next suspect."

I clenched my fist. "I'm going to question Sam and Irene Stringer next. If I find you there, I'll arrest you *both* for interfering in a police investigation."

"Do you hear that buzzing, Jace?" Glo chimed from his shoulder, taking a swig from her flask, glitter dotting her lips. "It's like an annoying gnat sound."

Jace laughed and turned away from me. "Don't worry, Detective. We'll stay out of your way."

10

I took a deep breath before knocking on Sam and Irene Stringer's door. I told myself if Jace and Glo were already here, I'd act professional. I wouldn't hex him, and I'd wait until we were alone before reading him the riot act.

The front door opened, and a middle-aged couple stood in the doorway. He was shorter than the woman by a good foot. His broad chest, muscled arms, and tan skin told me he still kept in shape by working outdoors. His hair was cut so close to his scalp, I couldn't tell its color. The tired, belligerent look on his face was more than just a man weary from hard work.

"Hello," the woman said.

She was a complete contrast to the lionfish shifter standing next to her. Where he was shorter and muscular, she was tall and willowy. Her shoulder-length brown hair and blue eyes complemented her smooth, pale skin.

"Mr. and Mrs. Stringer?"

"Yes," the sea witch said.

"I'm Detective Isla Ceartas. I'm the PADA detective now in

charge of the Bermuda Triangle. I'm investigating the death of Fredrick Longshore."

"Why?" Sam demanded. "Good riddance, I say."

"Sam," his wife softly chided.

"What?" Sam scowled at his wife. "Neither one of us is torn up about his death."

"What was that?" I asked, hoping Sam would clarify.

Sam scowled. "Nothing. Whaddya want?"

I heard the soft sigh from the woman, but she didn't chide her husband again.

"I'd like to ask you a few questions," I said. "Is now a good time?"

Sam's expression hardened, but he nodded. "Sure, Detective. Come on in."

I followed them into their cozy living room, taking a moment to glance around at the warm and welcoming decor. I was about to start with my line of questioning when a young woman descended the stairs. She had short blonde hair and wore traditional nurses scrubs.

"She's asleep," the woman said to Irene.

Irene looked at her watch. "So soon?"

"I know she has therapy in half an hour," the nurse said, "but I couldn't keep her awake. The stroll to the mailbox tired her out."

"That's okay," Irene said. "Thank you, Sara. We'll see you tomorrow?"

"Yes, I'll see you tomorrow. You guys have a good night."

The nurse gave me a curious look before nodding to me and exiting the house. When the door shut behind her, Irene gestured for me to sit down in the living room.

"Sara's one of our daughter's nurses," Irene explained.

"Is your daughter sick?" I asked, sitting on a sage green couch.

"Don't act like you don't—"

"Sam," Irene said, interrupting her husband. "She's new to the island. She honestly may not know."

I nodded. "I don't know the story. I only know what I've been told, and that's that you two had a problem with the deceased, Fredrick Longshore."

"One guess as to who told her," Sam muttered.

I was about to ask what he meant when Irene patted his hand. "Sam. I've told you a thousand times, it does no good to hold on to anger and bitterness. Let's just answer the detective's questions so she can get on with her day."

"I wanted to talk to you about your relationship with Mr. Longshore," I said. "I understand you had a dispute with him in the past?"

"A dispute!" Sam's jaw tightened, and he narrowed his gaze at me. "Yeah, I guess you can say we had a dispute."

"Can you tell me about it?" I prompted.

Sam pinched his lips together, and for a few seconds, he didn't say anything. "Almost two years ago, my daughter, Kristi, was hit by a car. Actually, both Kristi and Irene were hit by the car when walking across the street in town, but Kristi sustained life-threatening, permanent injuries." He looked away and swallowed hard. "And the bastard who hit them walked away with a slap on the wrist, thanks to Fredrick Longshore. May he rot in—"

"Luckily," Irene interjected, "the wonderful medical staff on the island were able to treat and heal Kristi as best they could—using both magic and modern medicine."

"It still didn't help," Sam said. "My daughter is paralyzed and has a brain injury. She pretty much needs twenty-four-hour care.

My daughter had her life ripped from her. One minute she's a happy-go-lucky jewelry maker who taught ballet to little girls on the weekends…and now she can't walk, feed herself without help, and even talking is a hardship for her. And is there any help for medical care? No. None. Meanwhile, I had to see Fredrick Longshore almost every day! Makes me sick! I'm just thankful the man who hit my family moved away so I don't have to see him." A muscle jumped in his jaw. "Otherwise, I don't know what I'd do."

I waited a beat before speaking, letting the emotions settle. "I heard there was a verbal altercation between you and Fredrick outside the courthouse."

Sam scoffed. "Yeah, we exchanged some words."

I turned my attention to Irene. "And you, Mrs. Stringer? Were you involved in the confrontation outside the courthouse two years ago?"

Irene shook her head, her expression composed. "I stayed out of it. I've never been one to resort to violence." The sea witch turned and smiled at her husband. "But we all deal with our emotions differently. I've come to accept that."

Sam Stringer hung his head. "I know I should do better, Irene."

Irene smiled and slipped her hand inside her husband's. "Dealing with grief is never easy."

"I understand that statement more than you know." I turned my attention back to Sam. "Mr. Stringer, you were also arrested about five months ago for hitting Mr. Longshore?"

Sam Stringer grinned. "Did a night in jail for it. Best damn sleep I've had since my daughter's life forever changed." He shook his head and looked away for a moment. After composing himself, he looked back at me. "I was angry. No denying that. The weight of our new reality. The medical bills alone…I let my emotions get the better of me. Fredrick ruined my daughter's life, and I wanted him to know how I felt. Nothing more."

I nodded. "May I ask where you both were last night from nine in the evening until seven this morning?"

Irene glanced at Sam before turning her attention back to me. "We were at home. We watched TV until around nine. After that, I went to bed."

Sam leaned forward, his gaze steady. "I stayed up until around eleven, just flipping the channels. I must have dozed off because I woke up around three in the morning. I went to the kitchen to get a drink before heading upstairs, and Irene was there making hot chocolate."

I couldn't help but raise an eyebrow at his detailed account. "Hot chocolate?"

Irene smiled softly. "It was actually a pumpkin spice latte." A soft blush rose on her cheeks. "I'm a little addicted to social media. My one vice. I posted my latte on Witchagram, if you want to check and see for yourself?"

I couldn't help but think the alibis for both suspects were a little too neat and tidy. "I'd love to see it."

Irene nodded and pulled out her phone, scrolling through her feed to find the post. She handed me the phone, and I read the caption: "October nights were made for pumpkin spice lattes. 🥤 🍪 #CozyMagic."

I handed the phone back to Irene. "Thank you, Mrs. Stringer."

Irene stood, her expression apologetic. "I'm sorry, Detective, but is it okay if we cut this short? Kristi's physical therapist will be here in twenty minutes, and I still need to wake her and get her ready for when he gets here."

"Of course," I said, rising from my seat. "I appreciate your time."

"I need to run to the nursery," Sam said, standing as well. "I have some last-minute things that need done before tonight's market."

"The Thursday Night Supernatural Market," Irene said. "We have a booth there where we sell our flowers."

"Oh, really?" I mused. "I've been meaning to stop by and check out the market, but I haven't had a chance yet."

"It's always the third Thursday of the month, from six to eight," Irene said. "Rain or shine. You should come out. It really is a wonderful community event. Local fruits and vegetables, flowers, artisans selling everything from baked goods to paintings to beauty products."

I smiled. "Thanks, I will."

Sam grunted and strode to the door. "Just so you know, Detective Ceartas, most supernaturals on this island aren't going to mourn the loss of Fredrick Longshore."

11

I pulled out of the Stringer driveway and headed back to town. It was going on four, so I figured Doc Bowers should be about finished with the autopsy. I'd just passed the welcome sign when my phone pinged. I pulled the Polaris over and read the text from Doc Bowers. She and Neil were finished and ready to go over results.

It didn't take long to get to the station, and the minute I opened the door, Nana pointed up the newly constructed stairs. "They're waiting for you."

"I'll be back down shortly to go over backgrounds, if they're ready."

Nana held up a stack of papers. "Got them right here."

I hurried up the stairs and into the brand-new labs. Like the downstairs, the upstairs was probably barely four hundred square feet. But it was big enough for both Doc Bowers and Neil to have state-of-the-art facilities.

Doc's lab was on the right, and Neil's was on the left. I opened Doc's door and stepped inside. I hadn't had reason to visit Doc's new lab since she moved over from Splash Island, so I was pleasantly surprised at the mix of modern-yet-hippie look. The autopsy table, instruments, and computers were brand new and sterile, but the colorful peace signs and other tie-dyed psychedelic artwork actually softened the harsh reality of what Doc Bowers did in the room.

"Love the room," I said.

Doc Bowers grinned. "Thanks. I find it helps balance both me and those I work on."

Neil nodded and pushed up his glasses. "Finding balance definitely helps with this job."

"How're you settling in?" I asked.

"Okay. I already have family wanting to visit." Neil shook his head. "The island may not be ready for them."

"You have a large family?" I asked.

Neil nodded. "Yes. Most crocodile shifter families are quite large. I have six other brothers and sisters. I'm in the middle."

"Wow," I said. "Being an only child, I can't image what that was like growing up."

"Loud."

Doc Bowers and I both laughed.

"Okay," Doc Bowers said. "Let's talk about Fredrick Longshore." She clicked a couple buttons on her computer. "Age, fifty-two. No serious health problems. Might have developed some liver issues later on had he lived and continued with current lifestyle. Broken leg from years ago, evidenced by the healing. Blood alcohol was right at the legal limit, but no illegal or prescription drugs were detected. As far as time of death goes, with magic, it's sometimes impossible to pinpoint. But taking into consideration everything, I put it between eleven and three. That's a *huge* chasm, I know. And usually I can get closer, but like I said, with magic, it's difficult."

"I totally understand," I said.

"Okay. Cause of death was heart failure, but the fact he'd shown signs of torture probably exacerbated the heart attack."

"What do you mean?" I asked.

"Enchanted seaweed was not only used to bind his hands and feet together, but I saw signs of strangulation as well. The physiological stress of that torture and near-asphyxiation, I believe, helped bring on his heart attack."

"I analyzed the net used to keep him bound," Neil said. "Traces of sea magic."

"Not too surprising considering where we're located," I said. "Not sure how that's going to help narrow down the suspects."

"This might help." Neil held up an evidence bag. "I found this in the cuff of the victim's pants."

"In the cuff of his pants?" I mused as I took the bag from Neil. "Is this a charm?"

"Looks like it," Neil said. "Ballet slippers."

It was all I could do not to dance a jig. I'd just come from the Stringers, and Sam had mentioned his daughter taught ballet on the weekends before her accident.

"I can work with this," I said. "Good work, Neil."

Using the camera on my phone, I snapped a picture of the charm and headed downstairs. The charm was a significant find. Maybe just the clue I needed to put the pieces together. The only thing better would be if Nana got viable leads as well.

I'd just hit the bottom of the stairs when I heard laughter. Looking over my shoulder, I saw Jace Solari sitting across from Nana—her flushed cheeks and huge smile left no doubt she was charmed by the devilish demigod.

"What're you doing here, Jace?" I demanded.

Glo zipped over to me, her signature flask in her claw. "Don't forget about me, Fishy Witch."

I rolled my eyes. "As if I could."

Glo grinned and tossed back the liquid elixir before smacking her lips and grinning. I narrowed my eyes at the glitter on her upper lip.

"Detective, so good to see you," Jace said, as though his presence was commonplace. "I was just being charmed by your lovely grandmother."

I pointed to the front door. "Out. Nana and I have work to do. We need to go over background checks."

"I'd love to sit in for that," Jace said, giving Nana a wink. "One former law person to another."

I snorted. "You were *never* PADA law enforcement. You may have bought some paper that said PI, but you're *not* law enforcement."

Nana waved her hand in the air. "Oh, pish! Let him sit in, Isla. Maybe he can tell us something we don't know."

"He's a *suspect,* Nana." I stared defiantly at Jace. "Or did you forget I told you to run his background?"

Jace grinned. "You had PADA run me?" He waggled his eyebrows. "I can't wait to hear what they had to say."

"Did you run my background?" Glo demanded. "Because it'll be filled with violence and horror. I can't tell you how many villagers I've burned alive with my fiery breath." She flew to Jace's shoulder, her scales and wings glowing purple and green. "The good old days when people cowered in fear and ran screaming from me."

I glanced at Jace to gauge his reaction. I never knew if the words coming out of Glo's mouth were truths or lies. Her size said lie...but her attitude said truth.

"If it helps," Jace said, "I have something germane to tell you. I promise, it will be a turning point in your investigation."

"I doubt that," I said.

Jace lifted his hand in the air. "Demigod promise."

I looked down at the infuriatingly charming man and studied him silently. Truth was, I didn't *really* consider him a suspect anymore. Not with the four or five I already knew who had much better motives. But there was just something so exasperating about Jace Solari that he put me on edge. I didn't know how to explain it or even what it was. "Fine." I pulled over the extra chair we kept in the office and dropped down next to Jace. "What have you got, Nana?"

"Lots of interesting stuff," Nana said as she lifted the first piece of paper and read. "Let's start with our victim, Fredrick Longshore."

"Ah, yes," Jace said. "The villainous lawyer."

I scowled at him. "New rule. You can stay, but you be quiet. I don't want Nana's or my attention diverted."

"Yes, ma'am." Jace mimicked locking his lips and throwing away the key. "My lips are sealed."

I closed my eyes and counted to five. "Okay, Nana. Go ahead."

Still grinning, my grandma looked down at the paper. "Fredrick Longshore. Fifty-two-year-old barracuda shifter. Been practicing law for twenty-seven years. He's divorced. No kids. No criminal record in either the human or supernatural courts. His finances were good. No major debt."

"Time of death was hard for Doc Bowers to pinpoint because of the use of magic," I said. "But she puts TOD between eleven and three. According to witness statements, right before Fredrick left the bar at nine-forty, he received a phone call. He's agitated, leaves the bar, says he will meet the person on the other end of the line in thirty minutes. That puts him at the north end of the island around ten-fifteen. Fits with time of death between eleven and three. There were signs of torture, so it very well could be he was tortured for a few hours before his heart finally gave out."

"Okay," Nana said. "Now, I have a sheet on Chester Montross. Says here he's thirty-seven. Unemployed as far as PADA can tell. A lionfish shifter. He's lived on the island his entire life. He's on his second marriage, but has no kids. He's got a pretty extensive criminal record…all of it in the supernatural court. There's two charges of B&E. One from five years ago, and the other from eight years ago. Looks like he did a month in jail each time. He's also had a misdemeanor assault charge that resulted in two weeks in jail and community service. Most recent was the possession of stolen goods. That was at the beginning of this year. He was sentenced to six months in jail. He just got out about two months ago. He's in debt up to his eyeballs." She looked up. "That's all I got."

I nodded. "Okay. So as far as Chester Montross' motive and alibi…we know he blamed Fredrick Longshore for the six-month jail sentence. Even though he was found with the stolen goods in his possession, Chester said Fredrick promised he could get him off with no jail time. Fredrick couldn't, and Chester went to jail. Chester also blamed the fact he couldn't find a job on Fredrick. We know from Celeste that Fredrick and Chester recently fought on the phone—"

"And me," Jace said.

I cut my eyes to him. "We know from Celeste *and* Jace that—"

"Ahem!" Glo said, her front claws crossed over her tiny, black body.

I rolled my eyes and threw up my hands. "Oh, for crying out loud! Fine! We know from Celeste *and* Jace *and* Glo that Fredrick and Chester had a verbal altercation on the phone, and then the bartender at Barnacle Bar & Grill told me the night of the murder, Chester Montross was in the bar. He and Fredrick had a physical altercation, and Chester left the bar around nine-thirty. Chester told me he went straight home and stayed there. I know that may be a lie because Jace told me a waitress told him she almost ran Mr. Montross over around one in the morning."

"And how did you get that info?" Nana asked Jace with a smile.

"I used my charms," Jace said.

Nana laughed. "I'll just bet you did."

"*Anyway*," I said. "If we believe the waitress, that means Chester Montross lied. He was wondering around on the island during the timeline of Fredrick Longshore's death."

"Next I have Wren Sellars," Nana said. "She's the ex-wife of Fredrick Longshore. She's a forty-eight-year-old mermaid. She's divorced with no kids. She moved to Neptune Oasis about twenty years ago. She's in debt, even though her spa seems to be doing well." Nana looked up from the paper. "I suspect the debt is because of her divorce. Anyway, no real criminal history except for tickets and that kind of thing."

"As far as her motive and alibi," I said. "Motive is obvious. She's bitter Fredrick got the house and really stuck it to her in the divorce. I went to her new place, and it was pretty shabby. She admitted it's a huge step down from where she used to live. She told me she had drinks with some girls at Sunken Vines Winery and then went straight home around ten." I shrugged. "Unfortunately, there's no one who can corroborate her statement. So she, too, has to be kept on our list of suspects. Especially since as a mermaid, she can wield magic, and seaweed wraps are her specialty."

"Next we have the Stringers," Nana said. "Sam and Irene. I'll take Sam first. He's a fifty-year-old lionfish shifter. Born and raised on Neptune Oasis. Married, with one adult child. He had no criminal record until recently. He was arrested about eighteen months ago in supernatural court for terroristic threats. He threatened to kill Fredrick Longshore outside the courthouse. He pled down to a misdemeanor charge. Then a couple months ago, he was arrested for assault & battery. He verbally threatened and then physically assaulted Fredrick Longshore. Did one night in jail and some community service. He and his wife own Neptune Oasis Nursery. There was no debt until about two years ago. Now, records show they are close to a hundred thousand in debt."

"And the wife?" I mused.

"Irene Stringer is also fifty. Sea witch. Married, with one adult child. No criminal record. Debt is the same as her husband's."

I leaned forward in my chair. "Okay. So until recently, Sam Stringer was my strongest suspect. When I spoke to Sam and his wife, Sam made no bones about his hatred of Fredrick and how he's happy he's dead. His wife tried on numerous occasions to get him to tone down his hate, but Sam wasn't having it. We know Fredrick defended the man who ran over both Irene and their daughter, Kristi. The result, according to Celeste, was Fredrick got the man off on a technicality because Irene and her daughter were jaywalking across the street. Sam told me his daughter used to make jewelry and teach ballet to kids on the weekends. Now she's paralyzed, has a brain injury, and has difficulty speaking."

"That's a big motive," Nana said.

"I agree," Glo said, taking a drink from her flask. "He sounds like the killer."

I shook my head. "I don't think so."

"Why?" Jace asked.

"Because of this." I yanked out my phone and brought up the picture of the ballet slipper charm, passing it to Jace. "Neil discovered this on Fredrick Longshore's body. In the cuff of his pants, to be exact."

Glo whistled. "So it was the mom. Makes sense. She can do sea magic. Case closed. Let's go arrest her and have a celebratory drink!"

I snorted. "Not yet. I still need proof. And I'm not saying she's the killer...I'm just saying—well, I don't know what I'm saying just yet. It's still processing."

Jace handed the phone to Nana, who handed the phone back to me. Slipping it back inside my pants pocket, I shrugged. "Now you understand why I think we may need to look at a female suspect."

Nana frowned. "You think we should eliminate Chester Montross?"

I shook my head. "Not yet, but I feel the ballet slipper is a huge clue we can't ignore."

"Who's next?" Glo asked. "I ain't getting any younger."

"Slow down," I said. "We still need to talk about alibis."

Glo rolled her neon yellow eyes. "Fine. Fine."

"Sam and Irene said they were at home watching TV until nine. After that, Irene went to bed and Sam stayed up to watch more TV. He fell asleep and woke up around three. Claims something woke him up. He went into the kitchen to get something to drink and his wife was in there making a pumpkin spice latte. She showed me a picture of what she posted on Witchagram. It was timestamped, so that's pretty solid, but it leaves Sam and Irene with no alibis from nine until three."

"Are you thinking they killed Fredrick as a couple?" Jace asked. "Or that only Irene did it?"

I shook my head. "I don't know. I mean, she's a sea witch who can wield magic. I can see a grieving mother finally taking matters into her own hands."

Jace nodded solemnly. "I can as well. I've dealt with thousands of grieving parents over my lifetime. When they feel like they have nothing more to lose, and their back is pressed to the wall, they will do anything to save their child."

There was something in Jace's tone that made me pause. Up until that moment, I'd just assumed Jace was an arrogant, devil-may-care kind of demigod. Someone who long ago lost sight of what it meant to care about another person. But that wasn't it at all. There was a story there. It wasn't the time or place for me to ask...but I definitely wanted to know.

"Next is Missy Weiss," Nana said. "Forty-six-year-old vampire. I show no marriages or children. Debt comes from the business she owns, Pearls & Pendants. No criminal record except for a disturbing the peace when she was nineteen. She received community service."

I sighed. "She'd only been dating Fredrick for a while, and I don't know of a motive. She seemed genuinely upset, just like Celeste Zephyr. She went to dinner with her aunt Wednesday night, then came home and had a Broom Chat conversation with her sister until around nine or ten. Then she went to bed because she knew Wednesday nights were Fredrick's nights with his guy friends. Thinking about the ballet slipper we found, I don't know how that would tie to Missy. I actually had Nana run her name because she's a girlfriend. I really have no reason to suspect her."

"Okay. Last person I have here is Celeste Zephyr," Nana said. "She's twenty-five. Part siren, part sea witch. Single, no kids. Her entire life has been spent on both Neptune Oasis and Splash Island. She has no criminal record, and the only debt she has is her car and credit card."

"I'm not sure why I had you run her background, either," I admitted. "I just wanted to get a read on all the players. I don't have a motive for her. She worked for Fredrick for a little over a year and a half. She seemed to genuinely like the man, even when others didn't. And as far as the ballet slipper clue is concerned, I have no idea how that would fit with Celeste."

Nana sat back in her chair. "That's all I got."

"What?" I sat up straight in my chair. "No way. Where's the file on Jace?"

"And me!" Glo exclaimed, leaping off Jace's shoulder. "I demand to know my dastardly deeds!"

Nana chuckled and shook her head. "Sorry, Isla. As far as PADA is concerned, Jace's file is confidential. And you're *really* not gonna like this next part."

I turned my head and glared at Jace. "What's the next part, Nana?"

"When I ran Jace's name through my computer here, I have nothing pending for him. No criminal matter at all."

"What?" I jumped up from my chair and slammed my fists on my hips. "What about the Diving in Restricted Waters charges?

Jace smiled. "Like I said earlier this morning, Detective. I doubt this ever goes to trial."

Myriad emotions flooded me. And I was sure they all showed on my face. I dropped back down in my chair, anger making it so I could barely focus. "What do you mean?"

"Let's just say PADA and I have an understanding. I do my own thing, but when they need something from me, I'm willing to do my part."

I jumped up from my chair again and paced in front of my desk. "So PADA *knows* you have the gold coin, and yet they are willing to look the other way because you *sometimes* help them out? That's BS!"

Glo snickered. "I think the Fishy Witch has her panties in a twist."

I stopped pacing and glowered at Glo.

"Are you trying to death-laser me?" Glo asked. "Because it's not working."

I lifted my hands, and I swear, I'd have zapped the snarky dragon a good one...had Nana not jumped up from her chair and captured my hands. "Now, Isla. There's no need to get violent."

"I'm not so sure about that," I growled.

Glo cackled, and her scales shimmered red and purple. "Bring it, sister!"

"There's more," Nana said.

"More?" I threw up a hand in exasperation. "What on earth could be next?"

"You might want to have a seat," Nana said.

Groaning, I dropped back down in my chair.

"PADA has suggested the two of you work together on this case." Nana smiled. "I think they feel if you two can work this out, then maybe Jace will hand over the gold coin he *may* or may not have found."

"Fat chance!" Glo exclaimed.

"I agree with the dragon," I said, crossing my arms over my chest. "Fat chance of us working together!"

Jace settled back in his chair. "I'm willing to give this a go. You know, since it's what *PADA* wants."

"I doubt you've ever done anything PADA wants," I said.

"Now that we're officially working together," Jace said. "Do you want to hear what else I learned today?"

For a few seconds, I just glared at the infuriatingly handsome demigod. But finally, common sense won out, and I sighed and uncrossed my arms. "Fine. What else did you learn on your unauthorized sleuthing today?"

Jace grinned. "I went on a dive near the west side of the island—"

"You can't—"

Jace held up his hand. "Are you going to chew me out, Detective? Or do you want to know what I learned?"

"Fine," I ground out. "What did you learn?"

He grinned. "I spoke–"

"Ahem!" Glo said.

"Oh, sorry," Jace said. "Glo and I spoke to a sea urchin named Spike."

I perked up at that. "I know Spike."

Jace arched an eyebrow. "You do?"

"Yes, she dates Needles."

"And who is Needles?" Jace asked.

"A flying and talking porcupine," I said. "He's partners with my friend, Shayla. So what did Spike have to say?"

"Well, it seems Spike couldn't sleep last night, so she decided to hang out in a lagoon close to where the murder happened. As she was swimming home, she saw what she called 'strange lights' on the beach. She swam as close as she could to see what was going on, but she stopped when she felt the dark magic."

"Did she see anything?" I asked.

"She saw a person. She couldn't make out for sure if it was a man or woman, or even what kind of supernatural it was, but she could feel the pull of powerful magic. Enough it scared her. She swam back home as quickly as she could."

I grimaced. "Darn. I can't exactly ask her what time she saw the person."

Jace chuckled. "Ahead of you, Detective. I asked her where she was exactly, and where the moon was overhead. By her response, I estimated it was between midnight and two in the morning."

I sat up straight. "You're sure?"

Jace nodded once. "I'm sure."

"Between twelve and two, we know Chester Montross was around because he beat on the waitress' hood around one. Both Sam and Irene Stringer admit to being up and in their house around three in the morning. If one or both of them were coming from the north end, that would be plausible. Wren Sellars, the ex-wife, is still up in the air because she was alone. Same with Missy Weiss and Celeste Zephyr. But at least we're narrowing the timeline down."

"So who are we staking out tonight?" Jace asked.

I blinked in surprise. "Excuse me?"

He chuckled. "Oh, come on. You forget, I used to be a PI. Of course you're gonna do a stakeout."

"My vote is this Chester Montross fella," Nana said. "See if you can't eliminate him all around."

I bit my lip. "I was thinking the Stringers."

Jace grinned and sat back in his chair. "No reason we can't do both."

"We?" I mused.

"Oh, yeah, Detective. We're in this together…partners."

The Thursday Night Supernatural Market transformed Neptune Oasis into a vibrant and mystical landscape. As I strode into the marketplace with Jace, I could smell the sea salt from the ocean air mixing with the glorious aroma of the food vendors. With the added touches of fall colors and pumpkins outlined in the backdrop from the stores, it was easy to see why supernaturals looked forward to the monthly festival.

Colorful tents lined the cobblestone street with myriad light orbs glowing in the air. Vendors sold everything from magical wares to exotic fruits and enchanted artworks. The first stall that caught my eye was a display of floating candles...their soft glow creating an ethereal ambiance that seemed to draw me and many other customers in.

The vendor, a tiny pixie maybe eight inches tall with iridescent wings that shimmered like a kaleidoscope of colors, chatted animatedly with a group of customers, each holding a candle cradled gently in their hands. The pixie's voice was musical,

JENNA ST. JAMES & STEPHANIE DAMORE

carrying hints of enchantment that seemed to echo through the air.

"Welcome, welcome, dear patrons!" the pixie exclaimed, her voice tinkling like wind chimes. "Behold the wonders of the Mood-Light Candles! Each candle is attuned to your emotions, changing its hue to match your innermost feelings."

A female werewolf shifter in the group raised an eyebrow, skepticism evident in her expression. "Emotionally attuned candles? How does that work?"

The pixie's eyes twinkled with mischief as she reached for a candle with a pure white flame. "Allow me to demonstrate." She held the candle aloft, her small hand enveloping the flame without harm. Slowly, the candle's soft, white glow began to shift, the light morphing into delicate shades of blue, reflecting the calm of a tranquil sea.

"See?" the pixie chimed, her voice a gentle harmony. "The candle senses your emotions and mirrors them. Calm and peaceful, just like the gentle waves of the ocean."

A murmur of amazement swept through the small crowd, but the woman's skepticism only seemed to grow.

"Oh, yeah?" the woman said. "What if I were to feel excited or joyful?"

The pixie's wings fluttered with excitement as she selected another candle, this one bathed in a warm, golden light. "Ah, excellent question! Observe." As the pixie's own mood seemed to shift to one of delight, the candle's radiance transformed into a vibrant and cheerful pink, reminiscent of cotton candy.

The werewolf shifter's impatience got the better of her, and reaching out, she snatched the candle from the pixie's hand. Instantly, the tranquil pink shifted and swirled, and the flame crackled with an angry, fiery red. The light flared and pulsed, casting an intense scarlet glow that seemed to throb with frustration and irritation. The woman's eyes widened in shock, and she dropped the candle as if she'd been burned.

As the pixie gracefully caught the falling candle and placed it back on the display, she shot the werewolf a playful yet knowing glance. It was as if her gaze held a hint of "I told you so" without uttering a word.

I couldn't help but snicker. "What was the werewolf thinking? Doesn't she know you don't antagonize a pixie?"

Jace chuckled. "She does now."

We continued down the iridescent cobblestone road. The booth next to the pixie's was a mother-daughter mermaid duo. The women sold stunning underwater paintings that came to life and moved and swirled on their own.

Even Glo seemed to be caught up in the allure of the market—although she'd never admit it, I was sure. Her wings pulsated with an electric green and yellow hue, mirroring the excitement she felt. Unfortunately, that meant her radiance was anything but inconspicuous. As she flitted from stall to stall, her scales shimmering with interest, I realized that her luminous presence could easily draw unwanted attention our way. And in half an hour, when the sun went down, it would be even worse because she'd turn into a glow-in-the-dark dragon.

"We need a disguise." I pulled Jace down the closest alleyway, away from prying eyes. "I want to blend in and eavesdrop without being recognized."

Jace's brow arched in curiosity. "What do you have in mind?"

"Think...typical tourists," I suggested. "Something that will make us go unnoticed in the crowd."

"I don't know," Jace said. "That seems a bit much, don't you think?"

"Oh, c'mon. Don't tell me the big bad demigod is afraid of a little spell?"

Jace narrowed his eyes, but I could tell he was amused. "I'm not afraid, Detective."

Before he could protest again, I whispered under my breath and conjured a glamour spell. I stifled a grin as I waved my hand in the air and visualized Jace's transformation. A faint pink light shimmered around him, transforming his appearance from his usual dashing self to a rather unconventional tourist. He sported knee-high socks paired with sandals, outrageously patterned shorts, and an oversized, loud Hawaiian shirt. His transformation was capped off with a pair of nerdy glasses perched on his nose. Gone was the captivating demigod. In his place stood an unassuming shrimp shifter.

As Jace blinked in surprise, I couldn't help but chuckle. "Now that's better."

His indignant expression as he stared down at himself only added to my amusement. "You're enjoying this way too much, Detective."

"I am. I really am."

Glo zipped down the alleyway...then caught sight of Jace and laughed so hard, she nearly tipped over backward. "Where's a camera when I need it? No one will ever believe this one."

Ignoring Glo, Jace lifted his finger to his face. "Glasses? Really?"

I turned my attention to my own transformation, altering my appearance into that of a middle-aged woman with a broad sunhat, oversized sunglasses, and a floral dress that screamed "tourist on vacation." I even added a faux fanny pack for good measure.

"At least you still look adorable," Jace grumbled.

"Ah, thank you!" Taking way too much pleasure in his grumbling, I wrapped my arm around his and propelled him out of the alleyway. It was time to gather information.

It didn't take us long to find the Stringers' booth. Glo flittered away to perch atop a tent, away from the crowd but still able to observe. Jace and I kept our voices low, adopting the hushed tones of genuine tourists as we exchanged comments about the vibrant array of stalls around us.

As we feigned interest in an enchanted bonsai tree that seemed to sway to an unheard melody, my ears remained attuned to the conversations happening around us. Gossip traveled like a gentle breeze, reaching our ears in snippets of hushed discussions.

"Did you hear about that Longshore fellow?" an elderly witch with a crooked hat whispered to her friend. "Seems like he got what was coming to him."

Jace shot me a sidelong glance, his nerdy glasses giving him an oddly endearing look. I nodded subtly, silently acknowledging I heard it too.

"Not a tear shed for that man," the friend agreed, her magical cane tapping gently against the cobblestones. "I hear there are quite a few who aren't too broken up about his demise."

As we continued to listen, a familiar figure strolled by— Celeste Zephyr. Sam and Irene were chatting happily with customers, arranging bouquets with genuine enthusiasm. However, when Celeste drew near, both Sam and Irene exchanged glances with each other. It was clear they were not happy to see the young siren-sea witch. Figuring it had to do with the fact she worked for Fredrick Longshore, I surreptitiously took a step closer to the three supernaturals.

"Hello," Celeste greeted with forced cheerfulness, stepping up to the Stringers' booth. "I was wondering if I could order some flowers for Mr. Longshore's funeral?"

"You dare come to our tent to—"

"Of course," Irene said smoothly, cutting off her husband's tirade. "We'd be more than happy to help you." Irene turned to her husband, the forced smile still in place. "Wouldn't we, dear?"

He grunted and turned away.

Irene pressed on. "Just let us know what you have in mind, Celeste, and I can write up an order for you."

Celeste nodded, and for a moment, the air felt heavy with unspoken tension. It was obvious Irene Stringer was putting on a polite front, but there was a definite undercurrent going on.

As if on cue, Fredrick's girlfriend, Missy Weiss, sidled up next to Celeste at the booth. Her eyes flickered briefly toward Celeste before landing on Irene and Sam.

I exchanged a quick glance with Jace, and we discreetly moved even closer, our disguises shielding us from any recognition.

Missy leaned in slightly, her voice hushed as she addressed the other three supernaturals. "Do you know anything about how the investigation is going?"

Celeste shrugged, though a hint of unease flickered over her features. "I know the female detective has been interviewing people. I've spoken with her a couple times. Seems like she's trying to piece things together."

Irene chimed in, her tone friendly but guarded. "Yes, she spoke with us too. Seems like she's casting a wide net, wanting to gather as much information as possible."

I arched an eyebrow at Jace. Did the fact Irene used the term "casting a wide net" hint at the enchanted net Fredrick had been tangled in when I found him?

Missy nodded. "I was interviewed as well. They're certainly being thorough, aren't they?"

The atmosphere grew awkward as the three women exchanged polite yet guarded remarks about their interactions with me. As they talked, I noticed their eyes occasionally flicking toward each other. Almost like they were searching for any signs of guilt.

"They suspect one of us is the killer," Missy Weiss finally said, her gaze shifting between Celeste and Irene.

"My money is on Chester Montross," Celeste offered with a knowing look. "He was always calling the law office and harassing Mr. Longshore. I told the policewoman that, too."

"I just hope she solves this soon," Missy replied, tears swimming in her eyes.

"How's Kristi?" Celeste asked.

Sam threw down the flowers he'd been arranging and whirled around. "Like you care? How *could* you—"

"Sam," Irene interrupted. "Do you want to help the next customer? Or should I?"

"You go ahead," Sam said, glaring at Celeste. "I need a minute."

I was so invested in the conversation between Sam, Irene, and Celeste that it took me a second to realize Irene was talking about me.

"Can I help you two with something?" she asked a little louder.

"Oh, sorry. Just looking," I said. "These are…unique."

"Those are Lumiphlox Noctis," Irene said. "Otherwise known as Moonlit Floret. They bloom only at night…that's why the petals are black right now. Tonight, the delicate petals will become luminescent and shimmer with shades of blues and purples. The center will open and tiny glowing specks reminiscent of stars will appear."

"That sounds lovely," I said. "I've never—"

I was cut off when Sam cursed loudly. "What's going on here?"

"What do you mean?" Irene asked.

Sam pointed to the top of a tent two booths over. "Isn't that the glow-in-the-dark dragon who's always with that nosey demigod? I hear he's been asking questions, too."

They all turned to look at Glo.

Celeste Zephyr fluffed her hair. "Guess that means the demigod is around."

Missy Weiss snorted. "Don't waste your time on someone like him, Celeste. He's a love-em-and-leave-em kind of guy. Trust me on that."

I had a feeling Missy Weiss had never spoken truer words.

"Maybe he just hasn't met the right woman," Celeste argued.

"Well," Irene said, "don't bring him a Silverflame Flower if you *do* get a date with him, Celeste."

"Why's that?" Missy asked.

"Yeah?" Celeste asked. "Why's that?"

"The Silverflame Flower is like a demigod's Achilles heel," Irene said. "While the Silverflame Flower can produce healing properties in most supernaturals, for a demigod, it causes paralysis and even weakness, if ingested."

"That's interesting," Missy Weiss said. "I had no idea it had an adverse effect on demigods."

"Me neither," Celeste said.

I held up the bouquet of Moonlit Florets. "I'll take these. But the Silverflame Flower sounds interesting. Do you have any on hand?"

Jace—AKA the nondescript shrimp shifter beside me—grunted. "Really?"

"Not here," Irene said. "But I have some at the flower shop."

I smiled. "Good to know."

13

I placed the Moonlit Florets on the backseat of my Polaris. "Something tells me this isn't the kind of place we'll find Chester Montross hanging out."

"Can you do a locator spell?" Jace asked.

"I could."

He grinned. "Detective, are you trying to do the next stakeout without me?"

"It's late. I'm sure you have other things you could be doing. How about I do this one on my own?"

Glo zipped down from Jace's shoulder and landed on the front seat of the Polaris, her scales glowing neon yellow and teal now that the sun had finally set. "Not on your life, Fishy Witch. We're in this together."

I sighed. "Fine. I'll do a locator spell."

I closed my eyes and concentrated on Chester Montross. Whispering the words I knew would bring him to mind, I focused on his physical location.

"What's the matter?" Jace asked. "You're frowning."

I opened my eyes. "I think he's either swimming or diving in the ocean." I locked eyes with Jace. "Not far from where you stole the gold coin."

"Allegedly stole the gold coin," Jace said.

I rolled my eyes. "Whatever. The question is, why is he there?"

Jace arched an eyebrow. "You're thinking he's looking for the fertility stone?"

I shrugged. "Weren't you when you stole the gold coin?"

"Allegedly stole," Jace automatically said. "Yes, we better get over there and see what Mr. Montross is up to."

"Are we flying?" Glo asked. "Or are we riding in this slow-moving turtle mobile?"

"Hey," I said. "My Polaris can hit up to forty miles per hour."

"Ooo," Glo mimicked, her colors changing to neon purple and green. "How exciting." Glo rolled her neon green eyes. "We better ride in the turtle mobile. Fishy Witch would probably lose her lunch if we showed her how to truly enjoy moving from one place to the other."

I told myself not to rise to Glo's bait, but between her snarky words and Jace's amusement...I couldn't help it!

"Fine," I said. "I'm game."

"Really?" Jace said. "You're good with me flying you?"

I swallowed hard, mentally kicking myself. This was something I'd never done before in all my forty years. "Of course. Why wouldn't I be? Unless you're too reckless for me to trust?"

To my utter shock, Jace reached up and ran his fingertip down my cheek. "You can trust me, Isla."

It was rare for him to use my given name. Usually he just called me detective in that mocking, I'm-more-superior-than-you way he had.

"Then let's go," Glo snapped. "I ain't got all night."

Her voice broke our connection, and I took a step backward. If Jace and I were going to work this case together, I was going to have to find a way to make the little jealous beast my friend. Otherwise, she might make it her goal to end me.

"What do I have to do?" I asked.

"Nothing," Jace said. "I'll do it all."

In the blink of an eye, he shifted into his dragon form. I couldn't help it...I took a step backward. He was absolutely magnificent and breathtaking. And totally intimidating. He had to be at least thirty feet long, from nose to tail, and at least twelve feet tall. His scales were a beautiful midnight blue with threads of silver running throughout.

He turned his massive head, and I met his glowing gold eyes. "Get on." His voice seemed to rumble from deep within his chest. "Just climb up."

"Won't I hurt you?" I asked.

He chuckled, and I swear, the earth under my feet moved. "Trust me, you won't hurt me."

I decided to levitate myself up. When I reached the top of his back, I straddled him the best I could and wrapped my arms around his neck. I pressed my chest against him, and I was sure he could feel and hear my heart racing and thumping in my chest.

"Hold on," Jace said, his voice reverberating throughout my body.

"Or don't," Glo said as she perched on the tip of Jace's massive wing. "Either way works for me."

I couldn't help it. The minute Jace spread his wings and took to the sky...I let out a squeak of alarm. Which seemed to amuse Glo to no end. Squeezing Jace tightly around his thick neck, I closed my eyes as we soared higher.

Thanks to Jace's enormous wingspan, it didn't take long to reach the beach where I'd first met Shayla Loci-Stone on her honeymoon. The moonlight cascaded and rippled across the water, giving the area an almost ethereal glow. Pirates Paradise—an actual pirate ship that was a resort and spa—was anchored in the water some twenty feet out.

The minute Jace's legs touched the sand, I levitated myself off his back and carefully descended. By the time I reached the sand, Jace was back in his human form.

"Well?" Glo asked. "What did you think?"

I nodded, not wanting to let on my stomach was still rolling in waves. "It was a lot of fun."

Glo rolled her neon green eyes. "Liar."

The sound of someone splashing out of the water had Jace and me spinning to see who it was.

Chester Montross stopped in his tracks when he saw us standing a few yards away. He tried to hide what he had in his hand behind his back, but Glo wasn't having it. She zipped over to the wide-eyed man and flew behind his back.

"He's trying to steal treasure!" she called out. "I say we shoot him for stealing!"

I didn't dare point out it was sort of like the pot calling the kettle black. She and Jace had done the same thing just weeks before.

"What?" Chester Montross exclaimed. "You can't shoot me! That has to be illegal."

"We answer to no one, you thieving lionfish!" Glo yelled, her scales glowing red and orange.

Hoping to diffuse the situation, I hurried over to where Chester stood.

"What have you got?" I asked, holding out my hand.

"It's not what you think," the man protested. "I was just going for a night swim when I saw something on the ocean floor. I went down for a closer look and found this." He held it up. "I don't even know what it is because I didn't get a good look at it. I wasn't trying to steal it. I was just going to bring it up here where there was more light. You know, so I could see what it was. I was going to put it right back."

The lies he kept spilling were so obvious, it was hard not to laugh.

Jace reached out and snatched the pottery piece from Chester. "If I had to take a guess, I'd say Staffordshire. Circa 1610, maybe?"

Our eyes met, and neither one of us said anything. I knew what that meant. The fertility stone PADA had sent me to find could be close. The stone went down in the Bermuda Triangle on the *Sea Venture*, an English ship that departed in 1632 for Jamestown in the Americas.

"Here's your one warning," Jace said. "Detective Ceartas and I are sworn to protect the treasures in these waters. You will cease and desist looking for anymore treasures in these waters." He took a step closer to the lionfish shifter. "Do you understand?"

Chester Montross nodded his head emphatically. "Yeah. Of course. Like I said—"

"That is all," Jace said in a tone that meant business. "You may go, and don't come back."

Chester Montross turned and all but sprinted across the sand.

"Look at you," I said, holding out my hand for the treasure. "Now you are sworn to protect the waters and treasures within?"

Jace grinned, and I saw the twinkle in his eyes. "Something like that. I thought it sounded nice and official, anyway."

"Maybe we should split the treasure?" Glo suggested.

I glared at the little dragon. "It's *not* treasure. It's an artifact that's been lost at sea. I will turn it over to PADA, and they will see that the rightful country gets the artifact back."

"As long as it's not been charmed, right?" Jace asked.

I smiled begrudgingly. "Right. As long as there's no magic attached to it. Then it goes straight to PADA to be squired away for safekeeping."

"I didn't detect any magic on that piece. Did you?"

I closed my eyes and focused on detecting any magic. "No." I opened my eyes. "I don't feel any magic."

Movement farther up the shoreline caught my attention, and I squinted to bring the figure into view.

"So now that I've proven myself trustworthy," Jace said, "I guess this means we continue with our current murder case tomorrow morning?"

The figure up ahead stepped out into the moonlight.

I sighed. "I suppose we do."

"The bakery tomorrow at eight sharp?" he asked.

I was about to tell him yes…when all the air seemed to rush from my body in one huge *whoosh*. For a few seconds, my vision blurred, the blood roared in my ears, and I swear the sand beneath my feet shifted and caused me to sway.

Or maybe I did the swaying.

"What's wrong with her?" I heard Glo say in that tunnel-vision way you sometimes get.

"Detective?"

I slowly came back to myself and the shakes settled in.

"Isla?" Jace cupped my face in his hands. "What's wrong?"

"Nothing," I whispered.

"Isla."

His tone was sharper this time, and I smiled. "You usually call me detective."

"Hey." He tilted my head up to meet his eyes. "What's wrong? You're shaking, and all the color has left your face."

I shook my head, tears filling my eyes. "It's nothing. I thought…"

"You thought what?" he prompted.

"I thought I saw my mom."

* * *

I told myself I'd just go for a quick swim. Get out of my head and let the magic of the water soothe me. It had taken a while to shake Jace from my side. It was sweet, really, the way he seemed to worry about me. But when I finally made it home, I bypassed the house I shared with Nana and went straight for the water. It was late enough no one was around on the beach.

Stripping down to my sports bra and underwear, I dived into the warm ocean water. The minute my body went under…my tail fin appeared, and I was immediately transformed into a mermaid.

Kicking my fin, I moved farther from the shoreline and deeper into the ocean. Since I was above the thermocline, I could see a school of iridescent fish swimming around a group of ancient sea turtles. Up ahead, a dolphin shot out of the water and then splashed back down into the depths of the sea, his cheerful clicks and whistles sounding like music to my ears.

Pushing down even farther, I immediately felt it when I went below the thermocline. The water was colder, and the area around me was dark and ominous. But this was also a part of the ocean I loved. For here was where the bioluminescent creatures lived. I spotted a couple jellyfish off in the distance, their long tendrils trailing behind them like strands of lights. They were headed for one of the many shipwrecks the Bermuda Triangle was known for. Any other night, I'd go say hi to the many sea creatures who lived inside the ships, but not tonight.

Tonight I just wanted to lose myself in the water. I didn't

even seek out Hydra Ann to say hello. Instead, my mind was consumed by the woman on the beach.

I swam for what felt like hours. I knew I needed to go back on land and talk with Nana about what I'd seen...but even that was causing me grief and heartache. Nana was going to be devastated. If it really *was* my mom, then that meant she'd intentionally stayed away all these years. Not caring how her disappearance affected us. Not caring about us at all.

As I pushed to the surface of the water and finally broke free, I sucked in a huge breath and slowly swam toward the sandy beach.

Which again made me think of the woman I'd seen. The woman who very well could be my mother.

14

"Good morning, Isla," Kyra Hayes called out as I strolled through the front door of Seashell Sweets Bakery the next morning. "Your usual coffee?"

The bakery was busy for a Friday morning, and I simply nodded my head, not wanting to shout to be heard above the din of the crowd. I saw Jace and Glo sitting near a window, but did my best to ignore them. I still needed time to myself.

Last night, after I'd walked into the house I shared with Nana, I'd wrestled with whether or not to tell her. After all, I wasn't even sure it *was* my mother. In the end, I told Nana what I thought I saw. Mainly because I never could keep anything from her. She could usually take one look at me and know something was wrong.

We'd stayed up for another hour, going over and over and over what I thought I saw—and why I thought it was my mother. After all, I hadn't seen her in person for almost twenty-five years, and the woman standing on the edge of the shore was at least twenty yards away in the moonlight.

But deep down in my soul...I knew.

In a way I could never explain...I knew.

I'd tossed and turned all night, and when the sun finally crested, I fell asleep for about an hour. Nana and I didn't talk about the possibility of my mom being in the Bermuda Triangle as we left for work—me to the bakery and Nana to the station.

By the time I made it to the bakery's counter, I was feeling more like myself. The immersion of water and sea life all around me in the décor helped to settle my soul.

"You're looking a little tired," Kyra said. "I hope it's okay I said that?"

I smiled. "It's totally okay. And I *am* tired."

She handed me my large cinnamon-vanilla latte. "What else?"

I shook my head. "I think this will do it."

Kyra frowned, and the cluster of stars tattooed on her temple magically changed colors. "No madeleine? Not even a simple scone?"

I smiled again. "Not today. My heart just isn't in it."

"You okay, doll?"

"I'm fine."

She leaned over the counter and hugged me. "When this case is solved, you and me will go swim in the ocean. Let our hair and fins down."

I stepped back from her embrace and laughed. "That sounds wonderful. How much do I owe you?"

She waved me away. "Get out of here. Go on about your day." She leaned in again and lowered her voice, the stars on her temple now a calming teal color. "The gossip mill is already running, so you might not want to stick around too long or someone will stop you and ask how the investigation is going."

I nodded and saluted her with my coffee. "Duly noted. I'll grab Jace and get out of here."

"And don't think you're not going to tell me about that!"

I rolled my eyes. "Don't ask."

"You get tired of that hardship...you send him my way." She winked at me. "I've never tried my hand at a demigod before."

Laughing, I said goodbye and strolled over to the table Jace and Glo occupied—avoiding eye contact along the way so customers wouldn't stop me.

"You ready?" I asked when I sidled up to their table. "Kyra suggests we head out now while we can."

Jace stood. "Before the locals beat us down for answers?"

"Something like that."

Glo tossed the last of what she had in her claw into her mouth and washed it down with whatever was in her flask.

"What's in the flask?" I asked.

"Why? You gonna bust my chops for it?" She demanded, her scales glowing red and purple. "Cops. Always gotta be giving law-abiding citizens a hard time."

"First off," I said. "You are *anything* but law-abiding."

Glo laughed and flew off the table, her scales now glowing yellow and green. "You got me there, Fishy Witch."

"What is it?" I asked Jace.

"Let's walk and talk," Jace said. "I can see the locals are getting restless."

I silently followed him and Glo out of the bakery, waving goodbye to Kyra.

"I was thinking we should go talk with Spike," I said as we slid into my off-road Polaris. "I'd like to hear for myself what she saw Wednesday night." I pressed down on the gas pedal. "And don't think I've forgotten my earlier question."

Glo settled down between Jace and me and crossed her front

claws over her chest, her scales now a fiery red. "Don't tell her, Jace. She'll just bust my chops."

"I'm going to need directions," I said.

"Back to the pirate ship," Jace said. "Spike lives not too far from the shore. Shallow enough we can wade in and you can do your thing and talk with her."

"How did *you* talk to her?" I asked. "Shifters can't hear all animals talk."

"Glo was my interpreter."

We rode in silence a bit more, and I wondered if I should press the issue about what Glo was drinking. I had my suspicions, and if I was right, I was going to put my foot down.

I parked my Polaris next to the golf carts Pirates Paradise Resort & Spa provided for their patrons. I could hear the faint strains of a guitar floating on the air as we strolled toward the beach along a narrow cobblestone path.

"That's Ren," Jace said. "He's a turtle shifter who likes to hang out by the boat ramp and serenade the tourists."

The path ended at the entrance of the beach. We were significantly closer to the pirate ship today than we were last night when we'd accosted Chester Montross. To my left was a wooden bridge designed to look like a large plank that tourists took to get onto the pirate ship. A vendor selling boozy ice cream was parked midway on the bridge calling out for customers and shooing away two seagulls trying to snatch his wares.

"Boozy ice cream at eight-fifteen in the morning?" I mused. "Isn't that a little early?"

Jace laughed. "These supernaturals are on vacation. It's never too early for booze."

A sandy-haired man in beach-bum attire strummed a guitar at the base of the bridge, his guitar case open to receive tips.

"Dude and Dudettes," he said, still strumming away. "So cool to see you. Little Glo, looking colorful today. Am I right?"

"Thank you, Ren," Glo said kindly.

I blinked in surprise. I'd only known the little she-devil dragon to be full of fire and spite. Hearing her almost embarrassed reply momentarily confused me.

"We're on our way to see Spike," Jace said.

"She'll totally dig that," Ren said. "I swam out to see her yesterday afternoon." He sent me a grin and a wink. "Ya know, after I baked a little in the sun."

I had a good idea what he meant by "baked" from his sheepish look and grin.

"She was totally shook, man. Hearing about the dead guy and all." He strummed his guitar quickly. "Left the little spiny dudette scared." He looked over his shoulder before leaning in. "Left me a little scared too. It's why I needed to bake in the sun. Still get nightmares about that day, man. We don't need another killer running around."

I suddenly realized who Ren was...and why he'd be having nightmares. He'd been caught up in the investigation Shayla and her husband had been working on during their honeymoon on Neptune Oasis last month.

"We're doing our best to find the killer," Jace said.

"Tubular, man."

Jace tossed a couple dollars into the open guitar case, much to Ren's delight. He continued serenading us with an island song as we slowly made our way over the sand and down toward the ocean's edge. We passed dozens of loungers already filled with tourists basking in the morning sun.

"I never thought to ask if Neptune Oasis stays busy all year round," I said. "Or if it slows down in the winter months."

"It's pretty much busy all year round," Jace said. "At least, that's what Ren told me. Around mid-January through March, it might slow a little, but otherwise, supernaturals want to escape all year round."

"So no heavy winters here?" I asked.

"Worst winters ever," Glo said from Jace's shoulder. "You'll probably hate it here, Fishy Witch. In fact, maybe you should pack up and move now?"

I rolled my eyes. "Nice try."

Jace chuckled. "Play nice, Glo. And as far as the snow and winter around here, from what I understand, it doesn't get too bad."

"Good to know. I'm not big on cold. I was raised on one of the Hebridean islands as a kid, and as I'm sure you know, Scotland can be like an iceberg."

We reached the water's edge, and Glo flew off Jace's shoulder. "I'll let Spike know we're here."

She zipped away across the water.

"It doesn't get deep?" I asked, kicking off my shoes and socks and rolling up my pant legs.

He chuckled. "Aren't you part mermaid?"

"I'm more worried about my clothes getting wet than drowning," I said dryly.

"You'll be fine."

Usually, when I stepped into the ocean water, I immediately shift into a mermaid. But since we were only going a short distance, I decided to stay upright on two legs.

The water was warm as it splashed around my calves. The grit of the sand and crushed shells felt good on the bottom of my feet as we headed toward a coral reef about twenty yards out.

"Spike lives between two brain corals," Jace said. "Not much farther."

By the time we reached Spike's house, the water was up to

my knees—soaking the bottom of my pants. The colorful sea urchin was floating topside, talking to Glo.

"Hello," the purple sea urchin said. *"My name's Spike. You must be the new law person."*

"I am. My name is Isla Ceartas."

"Mermaid?"

I nodded. "Part, yes. Part mermaid, part sea witch."

"Glo tells me you want to talk about what I saw the other night while swimming under the moonlight."

"I would, yes."

"Just tell her what you told me, Spike," Glo said, landing on Jace's shoulder.

"I couldn't sleep, so I went for a swim and to veg out at one of my favorite lagoons. It's a bit of a swim, but I wasn't tired. When I reached the lagoon, I just lounged and floated for a while. I remember the moon was almost overhead when I heard this sound. I swam out from the lagoon and around the cove and saw this strange light." The sea urchin's hard spines quivered. *"It scared me. Not something I'm used to. Then I saw a figure. It was yelling at someone or something I couldn't see. But I sensed the figure was angry. The magic they performed was dark. I could feel the evil."*

"Was it a man or a woman who was yielding the dark magic?" I asked. "Could you tell?"

Spike shook her head, her purple spines moving with her. *"No. I thought maybe female. They weren't large. Not like the demigod. And every once in a while I could hear the words, and it sounded female. But that was just a feeling. I never saw for sure."*

"Jace said he asked you where the moon was located in the sky," I said.

"Yes. I told him where it was as I was jetting home. I swam as fast as I could. I was that scared."

"Thank you, Spike. You've been a tremendous help."

The purple sea urchin smiled. *"Always glad to help. My boyfriend works for PADA as well. He helps Shayla and her husband, and soon he'll be traveling with Shayla's stepdaughter to solve crimes."*

"That's what I've heard," I said. "Quite the adventure he'll have."

"Luckily, my good friend, Ren, takes me into town once a week so I can do a Broom Chat with Needles. Otherwise, we'd never see each other anymore."

"What kind of relationship is that?" Glo demanded. "Long distance is never the way to go."

I scowled at Glo. "Maybe not for you, but for Spike and Needles, it seems to be working."

"Glo, I'm so glad you're here," Spike said. *"There's a rave happening tonight. You wanna stay and join me? And don't worry about where you'll sleep. There's a nearby lagoon we can swim to after the party, and you can sleep on the driftwood while I sleep in the warm water."*

"Stay behind now?" Glo asked.

"Oh, yes. We can make a girls' day out of it. I'm having a seaweed facial later today. I'm sure the girls at the salon can get you in as well. I'm also having my spines tipped with a glow-in-the-dark pink dye. It'll look killer with the glow of the moon under water."

Glo looked at Jace.

"What's going on?" Jace asked.

"There's a rave party tonight," Glo said. "Spike's invited me to stay and have a spa day, and then stay for the party tonight."

"Sounds like fun," Jace said. "You should stay."

Glo's scales shimmered red and blue. "Are you sure you can solve this case without me? I don't want to leave you saddled with an amateur." She looked pointedly at me. "She might get you killed."

I was about to tell her I was far from an amateur, but Jace laughed and shook his head.

"I doubt the detective will get me killed," he said. "After all, it's hard to kill a demigod."

"Trained professional," I muttered.

Glo looked between me and Jace...then to Spike.

"Okay," Glo said, her scales glowing purple and green. "I'll stay!"

"Girls' night! Gonna have a party!"

I laughed as Spike shimmied in the water.

"If anything happens to the demigod," Glo said to me, "I'll roast you alive."

To show just how serious she was, Glo turned her head and a stream of fire shot out of her mouth. Granted, it was only a foot or so long...but I could feel the heat where I stood.

"I had no idea you could do that, Glo!" Spike exclaimed. *"We should roast marshmallows tonight after the party."*

We said goodbye and headed back toward the shore. I thought about what Spike had said. I didn't want to lean too much on the fact she thought it was a woman yielding the dark magic, but it also went with the feeling I had Irene Stringer might be more involved than originally thought. I needed to find out if Irene had ever called the law office and threatened Fredrick Longshore, or if it was just Sam.

"I'd like to talk with Celeste again," I said.

"You doing okay this morning?" Jace asked.

"Yes, why?"

We stepped out of the water, and I quickly rolled my wet pant legs down and continued putting on my footwear.

"Because we haven't talked about what happened last night," Jace said. "You know, how you think you saw your mother. A mother who supposedly died almost twenty-five years ago."

"What do you know about it?" I demanded.

"Your grandmother told me a little when I was at the station yesterday."

"Save it," I said. "I don't have time to focus on that right now. Maybe after this case is solved, I can go there. But until then, please don't ask me to dredge up my past."

"Fair enough, Detective."

I needed to stay in the moment and focus on the facts. And right now, the facts were pointing me toward Irene Stringer. The connection to the ballet slippers charm was the biggest clue I had to work with.

🌿 15 🌾

The mid-morning sun bathed the quaint streets of Neptune Oasis in a warm glow as I drove through town. Figuring Celeste wouldn't be at the law office on Splash Island, I followed the GPS to Celeste's apartment on the east side of town. I didn't want to admit it, but I sort of liked having Jace beside me. I didn't like his rogue lifestyle or his careless attitude toward right and wrong...but I liked his presence.

"I've never asked you about your magical abilities," I said as I turned left at the intersection. "Do you have any magical abilities? Or any weaknesses I need to know about?"

Jace turned to look at me. "I have some magic on my mother's side—the dragon side. I can manipulate fire and smoke."

"What does that mean, exactly?"

"I can conjure both fire and smoke virtually out of thin air."

"Is that all the magic?" I asked.

"Courtesy of my great-great-great-grandfather, Apollo, I have the ability to heal, as you know. It's also my downfall."

"How so?" I asked.

105

Jace's jaw hardened. "Let's just say there's a reason I no longer use my healing capabilities."

I sighed. "I get that for some reason you don't want to tell me, but I *really* need to know. If we're going to be partners, I need to know the best way to protect you."

He grinned. "I can take care of myself, Detective. Demigod, remember?"

I narrowed my eyes. "Detective in Charge…remember?"

Jace sighed and stared at the road ahead of him, the wind tousling his hair. "Simply put, my ancestors were not happy with my cavalier attitude about healing. So about five hundred years ago, I was brought before Apollo and his council, and he cursed me, if you will."

"Excuse me? Your own great-great-whatever-grandfather *cursed* you because you were healing people?"

"Yes. So now, if I do something as simple as cure an illness or heal a serious wound, I am down for—oh, maybe a week or so for recovery. But it also takes about a hundred years from my life."

"So you can die?"

"I can die. There is no set date, of course. But I can die. As a demigod, I am vulnerable to certain things, unlike Apollo, who is immortal."

"This is so fascinating. Okay, so now I know why you've stopped being a healer and now steal treasure for a living."

"Allegedly steal," Jace said smoothly.

I rolled my eyes. "Allegedly steal."

"And if I heal someone who is slated to die…well, let's just say I've been told I may not like the outcome."

"Why?" I whispered.

Jace chuckled, but there was bitterness laced in the laugh.

"Not only will I be punished for it, but I will lose up to a thousand years for such an insolent act."

"I don't understand," I said. "I thought your gift was healing. Why wouldn't Apollo want you to use it?"

Jace smiled wistfully. "Sometimes, when you know you cannot die in a reasonable time like everyone around you, and you are cursed to walk the earth for thousands and thousands of years, you can take that frustration out in many ways. For me, I slapped back by healing everyone around me, even people I didn't know. I figured if I couldn't die, then they shouldn't die. I was not healing for anything other than spite."

I placed my hand on his arm. "I'm sorry. I had no idea that's why you'd stopped healing. Or were told to stop healing. It was wrong of me to assume it was…"

"What? That I stopped helping others because I wanted to hunt treasure instead?"

I shrugged, released his arm, and gave him a small smile before turning back to the road. "Something like that."

We sat in silence for a moment.

"What makes you vulnerable?" I asked. "I mean, is it true what Sam said last night about the Silverflame Flower?"

"Are you planning my demise, Detective?" He grinned, showing me his dimple. "Just so you know, I'm not that easy to kill."

I rolled my eyes. "Don't be ridiculous. But I need to know."

Jace nodded. "Okay, then. Yes, crushed petals from the Silverflame Flower can be disastrous to all demigods. I'm also especially vulnerable to Dragon's Tears."

"Dragon's Tears," I said. "Really?"

"Yes. Whereas it can be used in spells to heal supernaturals, like the Silverflame Flower, the Dragon's Tears can weaken me and make me vulnerable."

"Fascinating."

I turned right and pulled into Celeste's apartment complex. Finding the first vacant spot, I parked the Polaris, and Jace and I strode toward the three-story yellow stucco building. The swaying palmettos offered plenty of shade along the cobblestone walkway.

Celeste lived on the second floor, so we took the stairs side-by-side. I located her apartment number and knocked on the door. A few seconds later, Celeste opened the door…and her eyes widened in surprise when she saw Jace.

"Oh, well, this is an unexpected visit." Her cheeks flushed as she fluffed her hair. "What can I do for you, Mr. Solari?"

"Good morning, Celeste," Jace greeted with a casual smile. "Apologies for the early hour, but we could use your help."

"Of course, anything." Celeste stepped back and motioned us inside. "Excuse the mess."

I glanced around the room. Not a single thing was out of place. Not even a dish in the sink, from what I could see. Celeste pushed a button on her phone, and the music that had been playing softly in the background stopped.

"Have a seat, please," she said.

As we settled into the cozy living room, I directed the conversation toward our investigation. "We're just checking to see how you're holding up?"

"I'm okay. A lot of people who see me out in public are really nice and tell me they're sorry for what happened to Mr. Longshore." Tears filled her eyes. "And that's really nice." She let out a soft chuckle. "But not everyone is so kind. Donald Warner's ex-wife stopped me in the grocery store yesterday afternoon and read me the riot act. Margo was *not* happy."

I frowned. "Margo? She's the ex-wife of the man Fredrick

Longshore met earlier in the evening on the night he was murdered?"

"Yes. She told me she was glad Mr. Longshore was dead. She said maybe now her husband wouldn't be protected and would start paying her the money he owed."

I exchanged a glance with Jace. It looked like we'd be heading to Margo Warner's house next.

"I wanted to ask you about Irene Stringer," I said.

"Irene?"

"Yes. I assume you know her?" I asked.

Celeste nodded. "Oh, yes. They aren't happy I took a job with Mr. Longshore, but I have to pay my bills."

I frowned. "They aren't happy with you because of what happened to their daughter?"

"Yeah." She looked away and shrugged. "But I did what I thought I had to do. What I thought was right."

"Let's talk about Mrs. Stringer," I said. "Has Irene ever called the law office and threatened Fredrick Longshore like Sam?"

Celeste furrowed her brows. "Irene? I'm not sure. Maybe, but I can't—I don't think so. Mainly it was Sam."

I tried not to show my disappointment at her answer. I was sure I'd been on to something with Irene Stringer.

"Thank you for talking with us," I said. "I hope we didn't interrupt your morning."

"Not at all. I'm out of a job right now, so I have plenty of time."

"Give it time, Celeste," Jace said. "Something will come around."

Nodding, Celeste stood, and we followed suit, walking toward the door.

Just as we were about to leave, Celeste cleared her throat and cast a slightly nervous glance at Jace. "Mr. Solari—Jace. I was wondering...perhaps we could catch up sometime? Maybe for a drink or dinner? Just the two of us?"

Jace's response was gentle yet firm, a warm smile on his lips. "I'm sorry, love. But this one has me in a ball-and-chain." He wrapped a hand around my arm. "You understand?"

I yanked my arm away, my cheeks flushing with irritation. "Don't be—"

"Oh, I didn't realize," Celeste stammered, embarrassment and disappointment coloring her features. "Never mind, you two have a great day. Sorry about that." She quickly slammed the door, leaving us to stare at the closed door.

As we walked away from Celeste's apartment, I turned to Jace and scowled. "Why did you do that?"

Jace met my gaze, his expression serious. "It was the kindest way to turn her down."

I huffed in frustration, my irritation not fully abated. "Well, just remember that we're here for business, not for personal encounters."

Jace chuckled softly, his eyes twinkling with amusement. "So now's not the time to ask you out for dinner?"

"Be serious."

"I actually was. I think we should have dinner one night soon. I make a mean mango shrimp taco."

"Not happening, Demigod."

We settled into the Polaris, and I pulled out of the parking lot.

"By the way, Detective. What did you think of her choice in music?"

"What?" I asked, turning left onto the street.

"Celeste's choice in music. Didn't you recognize it?"

I frowned. "No. Why would I?"

He chuckled. "Not a fan of the ballet?"

I jerked the Polaris to a stop. "Excuse me? What about ballet?"

"The music was from *The Firebird* by Igor Stravinsky."

"How do you know that?" I asked.

"I've been around more years than you can imagine, Detective. I've seen a lot of things in my lifetime. I actually enjoy the arts. Opera, ballet, musicals, and even stage plays."

I'd think about that later. Right now, I needed to figure out how Celeste Zephyr might somehow fit into the puzzle of who murdered Fredrick Longshore.

If she fit at all.

I plugged Margo Warner's name into the app I had, and after a few tweaks, I pulled into her driveway fifteen minutes later. I recognized the area of town we were in. Market Road was definitely in the seedier part of town. Most of the houses and businesses along the street were run down and dilapidated. A few even had bars on the windows.

A sad-looking scarecrow surrounded by miniature pumpkins was propped against a tree in the front yard. A pink and yellow bike lay on its side as I walked up the front steps. I knocked twice, then stepped back next to Jace.

The door opened, revealing a tired-looking woman with worn features. Her hair was pulled up into a messy knot high on her head, and her clothes were wrinkled and stained.

"Can I help you?" she asked, her voice tinged with apprehension.

"My name is Detective Ceartas, and I'm the new PADA detective for the island. This is my civilian consultant, Jace

Solari. We'd like to ask you a few questions regarding the murder of Fredrick Longshore."

Margo's gaze flickered between the two of us before she nodded, opening the door wider to allow us entry. As we stepped inside, I noticed a young girl of about four or five sitting in the living room, engrossed in a cartoon.

"We can talk in the kitchen," Margo suggested, leading us to a small but tidy space where we could have more privacy. "Can I get you something to drink? Coffee, maybe?"

"We're fine," I said.

"I could use some," Margo said. "Is that all right?"

"Of course," I said. "Go right ahead."

"I'm so tired lately, and this is the only thing keeping my head above water." She shuffled over to the coffeepot and poured the hot liquid into her mug before returning to sit at the table. "I guess I can't say I'm surprised you're here." She blew across the mug and took a small sip. "I've been pretty vocal about how mad I am about my ex-husband and Mr. Longshore."

"Why don't we start there," I said. "Tell us about that."

"My ex-husband is an accountant," Margo said. "We were married for seven years before he filed. Like most divorces, one person usually comes out ahead over the other. In this case, I was definitely the big loser. I didn't even get to keep the house. That's for him and his new wife. I never even saw the money I was supposed to get for the equity. That's 'tied up' somehow." Her chin trembled. "I'm supposed to get six hundred a month to help with child support, and I can't even get that from him most months!" Tears filled her eyes. "Donald makes a lot of money. It's not like he can't afford six hundred dollars for his daughter. In fact, I should have gotten more like a thousand, but it didn't happen. That's why I've been calling and harassing Mr. Longshore." A tear slipped down her cheek. "I'm just so *frustrated* and angry! I have bills piling up, and nothing I can do about it. I wanted Mr. Longshore to put pressure on Donald to pay me, but I didn't really think it would happen." She rolled her eyes. "They were childhood friends. One snake friending another."

"I'm sorry," I said. "That definitely doesn't sound fair."

"Thank you. My mom tries to help as much as she can."

"I need to ask you about Wednesday night," I said. "Can you tell us where you were Wednesday evening, from nine until seven in the morning?"

Margo sighed, her tired eyes meeting mine. "I'm a nurse at St. Seabreeze Hospital. I work three back-to-back, twelve-hour shifts usually. Wednesday night, I got off a little after midnight, clocked out, and then stopped by the all-night café for a bite to eat before driving home."

"Makes for long nights," Jace said.

"It does," Margo agreed. "But I love my job."

I leaned forward in my chair. "Can you give us an approximate time you arrived home?"

Margo considered for a moment. "I'd say around one-fifteen or one-thirty. My mom stays here and watches my daughter for me on nights I work. She just stays overnights."

"So you got home around one-thirty," I said, making a note of the timeline. "Could your mom corroborate your statement?"

Margo's expression shifted to one of frustration. "Probably not. It's not like she stays up and waits for me to get home. She puts Miranda down for bed, and then she goes to bed shortly thereafter. She doesn't wait up for me." Margo looked over our shoulder, through the doorway to where her daughter was still presumably watching TV. "So, no. I don't think anyone could corroborate my statement. I didn't—"

"Mommy, mommy!" the little girl cried as she hurried into the room. "Can I have Goldfish? Please? Please?" She jumped up and down, her purple and yellow tutu moving with her. "Hurry! Hurry!"

Smiling, Margo got up and placed her hand on her daughter's head. "Just a couple. I'll fix you lunch soon."

"Okay." The little girl turned to look at Jace. "Hi. You're big. My name's Miranda. I'm four. I sometimes go to pre-school. But not today. Are you in school?"

Jace chuckled. "I haven't been in school for a long time."

"Oh. So you're like Mommy? You save people and heal them?"

Jace rocked back in his seat, a stunned expression on his face. "Well, I used to."

"Miranda," her mom chided from the counter. "Don't bother the nice man."

"It's no bother," Jace said. "I used to help heal people, but I haven't done that in a long time."

"Why not?" Miranda asked, jumping up and down, her tutu bouncing with her. "You didn't like it?"

Jace frowned. "It's not that I didn't like it, but more…" He trailed off. "Well, let's just say it took a lot from me, and after a while, I decided I didn't want to do it anymore."

The little girl put her two small hands on Jace's knee. "I'm sorry."

Sorrow and a couple other emotions I couldn't put my finger on flittered across Jace's face. He smiled at the little girl, but I got the feeling he was hurting. Not something I thought the arrogant demigod was capable of.

"Thank you." Jace patted her hand. "I like your dress."

Miranda giggled and twirled, sending the tutu fluttering out from the green leotard. "It's not a dress, silly. It's a tutu. Mommy takes me to a place to dance."

"Here you go." Margo waved her hand in the air, and a plate

of Goldfish crackers magically floated over to her daughter. "Go take them to the other room and watch TV."

"Okay!" The little reached out and caught the plate. "Bye!"

No one said anything until the little girl scooted out of the room.

"I hate to disappoint her," Margo said as she shuffled back over to the table, "but the truth is, I can't afford to keep her in ballet anymore. She's asked when she can go back, and I've been making excuses." She sat down at the table and took a huge gulp of her coffee. "I understand why you have to ask my whereabouts on Wednesday night, but trust me, Detective Ceartas. If I had the energy to kill someone, it wouldn't be Fredrick Longshore. It would be the man who will no doubt continue to disappoint my daughter—his own flesh and blood—for many years to come."

Margo looked away as her words hung in the air. I couldn't help but feel the weight of her pain and frustration, but that just gave her a bigger motive as far as I was concerned. And when you added in the fact her daughter danced ballet, and that Margo was in town alone during the time of the murder and could obviously wield magic...I simply couldn't discount the fact Margo Warner could be our killer.

"Thank you for talking with us." I stood and nodded to Jace. "We'll get out of your hair so you can fix your daughter some lunch. We can show ourselves out."

When Jace and I reached the front door, the little girl turned around from the TV and stood, grinning at Jace. "Maybe you can come see me dance sometime?" She twirled. "I'm real good."

"Maybe I will," Jace said, winking at the girl. "I love the ballet."

I opened the door and hurried down the stairs to the Polaris. I didn't want to admit it, but it broke my heart knowing Miranda wouldn't be taking ballet lessons anymore simply because her father refused to keep up with child support payments.

"I feel like finding Donald Warner and giving him a piece of my mind," I grumbled as I pulled out of the driveway.

Jace smiled, but it didn't reach his eyes. "I wouldn't worry too much about it, Detective. These things have a way of working themselves out. I bet this time next week, Miss Miranda will be twirling about in ballet class."

There was such a truth and finality to his words, I didn't question it.

"Just don't leave a mark," I said. "I don't want to arrest you."

Jace turned to me and grinned. "Why, Detective, whatever do you mean?"

My cell phone chirped from my pants pocket. Yanking it out, Nana's face appeared on the screen. Sliding my finger over the icon, I put her on speakerphone.

"Hey, Nana. What's up?"

"Call just came in. Seems someone just broke into Fredrick Longshore's house."

🐾 17 🐾

"I don't like the looks of this," I said as I levitated myself off Jace's back.

Fredrick Longshore's front door was open, and a moped sat parked in the circle driveway of the sprawling two-story limestone house and professionally manicured yard.

"Any idea who it belongs to?" Jace asked after shifting back to human form.

"Nope. Those are the mopeds all three islands give out to tourists. Stay behind me and follow my lead."

Jace grinned. "I'm aware you're in charge, Detective."

"Excuse me! Stop right there!" a shrill voice called out.

I turned and saw an elderly woman with a cane hobbling our way.

"You stop right there!" she hollered. "I've had enough of this nonsense. That man might be dead, but you can't just go wandering in places you don't belong." She came to a stop in front of me, clearly out of breath, and lifted her cane in the air. "You young folk have no respect!"

"Ma'am," I said. "I'm the new PADA detective for the Bermuda Triangle. This is my consultant, Jace Solari."

"Cops, you say?" She lowered the cane. "Well, why didn't you say so? It's about time!"

Jace laid a hand on the woman's arm. "Why don't you tell us what has you so worked up?"

"I'll tell you what has me so worked up. Last night, I couldn't sleep, so I get up and shuffle to the kitchen for a spot of tea and a dash of brandy. I look out my window, and what do I see? Lights! Lights on over here in this house. I was about to come over and give the person what-for, but by the time I got my coat on and found my walker, the lights were gone."

"You should have called the island's emergency number," I said. "Dispatch would have contacted me on Neptune Oasis, and I'd have come out."

She looked me up and down. "And how would you have gotten here quickly? I sense sea witch and mermaid. You gonna speed swim over from Neptune Oasis?"

Jace chuckled, and I wanted to give him an elbow to the solar plexus.

"I can shift and fly, ma'am," Jace said. "I could have flown her here."

I sucked in a breath. Was that why PADA wanted us to work together? They thought my inability to get somewhere quickly between the islands was a hindrance? If so, then why didn't they just send me a shifter partner who could fly? Why did I have to be momentarily partnered with the exasperating demigod?

I gave myself a mental shake and focused on the older woman. "Do you know what time you saw the lights last night?"

"Dunno. I guess sometime after midnight." She pointed her cane toward Fredrick's house. "And then this girl arrived about twenty minutes ago, so I called the police and was on my way over when I saw you two."

"It's a girl inside?" I mused. "You're sure?"

The elderly shrimp shifter narrowed her eyes at me. "You sayin' my eyesight's too bad to tell?"

"No, ma'am. I just—never mind." I gave her a small smile. "Thank you for letting us know about last night. We'll take it from here."

The woman grunted, turned, and hobbled back across the street.

I glanced at Jace. "Like I said earlier, stay behind me, and follow my lead."

Jace winked. "I've got your backside, Detective."

At my glare, he cleared his throat.

"I mean, I have your back, Detective."

Preferring to use my magic over a weapon, I strode up the front steps and peeked inside the open doorway. "This is Detective Isla Ceartas with the Bermuda Triangle PADA Department. I'm coming in."

No sooner had Jace and I stepped inside the foyer than Fredrick's ex-wife, Wren Sellars, appeared in the entryway.

"Hello, Detective," she said. "What are you doing here?"

"I can ask you the same thing."

"Missy Weiss called me all upset this morning. There are some personal items she left here that are important to her, and so she asked me to retrieve them for her." Wren shrugged. "I still had a key Fredrick didn't know about, so I figured now was a good time to see if it still worked."

"You shouldn't be in here," I said.

Wren snorted. "Why? Are you afraid I'll take something from here that belongs to me? Trust me, I can find plenty. Fredrick screwed me over big time, but I'm not here to get revenge. I'm here to get Missy the closure I never got by retrieving items she left behind."

"That's not really your call," I said. "Out of curiosity, were you in this house last night?"

"Last night? No, why?"

"No reason."

"I suppose I should have just called Celeste." She held up the items in her arms. "I'm done here. Do you want to go through these items to make sure it's all stuff that belongs to Missy?"

I glanced down and saw a couple blouses, a hairdryer, and a makeup bag. "No. But I would like to ask you how Celeste Zephyr got the job as secretary."

"Celeste?" Wren shrugged. "Fredrick needed a new secretary when the one he previously had, a seahorse shifter, died in her sleep."

"How old was she?" I asked.

Wren smiled. "Old. I'd say maybe mid-nineties. She'd been with Fredrick since he returned to Neptune Oasis and opened his law firm."

So much for thinking foul play might have been involved. Mid-nineties was elderly, even for a shifter.

"We need to look around," I said. "I'm going to ask you to leave, please."

"Sure thing." Wren started for the door, then stopped. "Oh, hey. I'm not sure, but I think someone has been in the house."

"Besides you?" Jace asked.

Wren grinned. "Yes, besides me."

"What makes you say that?" I asked.

"Fredrick was diligent about the safe he kept in his office. He changed his password every month." She held up a hand. "And before you read me the riot act about snooping around in his office, I don't care to hear it. You have no idea how bad things really were toward the end. Anyway, I went into his office, and the safe looks like it's been dropped through a gigantic shredder. It's all banged up."

"Still locked?" Jace asked.

"Yep. Locked up tight."

"Thank you," I said. "We'll look into that."

"See ya."

Jace shut the door behind Wren and turned back to me. "What are you thinking?"

"I can't decide if it's Irene Stringer or Margo Warner who's our killer. But I think it has to be one of them. Both have an obvious connection to the ballet, and both need money. So it has to be one of them."

"Or both?" Jace asked.

"Accomplices?" I shrugged. "I can't see it. At least, not yet. What would bring the two women together? Why would they join forces to kill Fredrick Longshore?" I turned and looked around the foyer. "In a house this size, finding the study may take a couple tries."

"Should have asked Wren where it was."

I laughed. "Right. Okay. You take upstairs, and I'll take downstairs. Holler if you come across the study with the safe."

I wandered through the kitchen, living room, formal living room and dining room before finally stepping into the study. A large mahogany desk with towering bookshelves on either side dominated the middle of the room. A tattered leather couch with cracks and worn spots sat against one wall, a bronze floor lamp next to the sofa. On the other side of the room stood a five-foot metal safe. I was about to text Jace when someone cleared their throat behind me.

Whirling, I glared at Jace standing in the doorway. "You scared me!"

"I was just going to let you know there were only bedrooms, bathrooms, a laundry room, and an entertainment room upstairs." He stepped into the room beside me. "But I see you found it."

"I found it."

Jace and I strolled over to the safe and examined it from all sides.

"It's definitely had a crowbar or hammer taken to it." I said.

The surface of the safe was bent and warped in various locations, and even one hinge and the locking mechanism had been smashed beyond repair.

"Not sure what we're going to get from this," Jace said.

"Nothing," I said.

Even I heard the disappointment in my tone.

I was about to suggest we go...when something under Fredrick's desk caught my eye. Grabbing a latex glove from my back pocket, I squatted down and picked up the object on the floor.

"Well," Jace said. "That should narrow it down some."

I turned the crushed flower petal over and examined the back side. There were no discerning marks to tell me where it came from, but I thought it too coincidental for it not to be from Neptune Oasis Nursery—Sam and Irene Stringer's place.

I conjured up an evidence bag and was about to suggest we go when my cell phone rang. Handing the bag to Jace, I pulled out my phone and answered, putting her on speakerphone.

"Hey, Nana. What's up?"

"Emergency call just came in from a Sara Wifton. She's a nurse for Kristi Stringer. She found Sam Stringer on the floor in Kristi's room. She thought he was dead at first. She was able to revive him, but he's still out cold. Ambulance is on the way. No sign of Irene Stringer."

My eyes met Jace's. "We're on our way."

"One more thing," Nana said. "I guess the daughter can't really talk, but she can communicate enough the nurse can understand her. The nurse said the daughter was hysterical and kept repeating the sound that meant 'mom' over and over again. Just thought you'd want to know."

"Thanks, Nana. Jace and I are on it. I'll check in later."

I disconnected the phone and shoved it in my pants pocket. "Why would Irene attack her husband in her daughter's room?"

"Only way to know is to ask. Can you do a locator spell?"

"Yes. As long as she hasn't done a cloaking spell to hide herself."

Jace nodded. "Let's hope she's too distraught to have thought of that."

I closed my eyes and whispered the locator spell I'd learned years ago. It didn't take long before images of flowers and a greenhouse bombarded me. The smell of fragrant flowers and wet earth permeated my senses.

I opened my eyes. "She's at the nursery."

"Let's go. I can get us there in under ten minutes."

"Land us as close as you can to the brick building," I said.

Jace nodded his massive head and dipped slowly to the ground. As we glided past the trees and entrance to Neptune Oasis Nursery, I thought about my plan of action. I needed to confront Irene and get her to confess to killing Fredrick Longshore and attacking her husband.

As I levitated myself off Jace, he shifted back to his human form.

"Again, stay behind me," I said as my feet touched the ground. "I have magic, and I have my Binder."

"Ah, yes. The magical device that encases a rogue supernatural and strips them of all magical powers."

I arched an eyebrow. "You say that like it doesn't work on demigods."

Jace grinned. "It doesn't."

"Even still," I said. "You follow me."

"Of course, Detective."

He was being a little too agreeable, but I didn't have time to worry about it because I had a killer to apprehend. I strode up the walkway, toward the front of the brick building. In the background were four large greenhouses and acres of trees. Putting my finger to my lips, I gestured for Jace to be quiet.

I grabbed the handle to the glass door and slowly opened it—careful not to make a sound. When I heard the soft click of the door behind me, I knew Jace was inside as well.

Glancing around, there were two doors inside the foyer, one on each side of the room. Voices carried down the hallway from the door leading to the right. I motioned my head, indicating I was going to the door. Jace nodded once, and I hurried through the doorway and down the hall.

"Where is it?"

I stopped when I came to another open door. I thought I recognized the voice inside, but it didn't make sense. Frowning, I peeked inside and saw two figures standing next to a desk in the middle of an office.

"Where is it?" Celeste Zephyr demanded again.

"I don't know." Irene rummaged around in the desk drawer, then slammed it shut. "I usually keep Kristi's bracelet in here. I must have taken it home."

"I already looked!" Celeste exclaimed. "It wasn't in your jewelry box or Kristi's."

Irene whimpered. "Why are you doing this, Celeste? You were Kristi's best friend! Why would you betray her this way?"

"I did this for you guys!" Celeste screamed, yanking Irene away from the desk. "I did it for Kristi!"

"Stay here," I mouthed to Jace before stepping into the room.

"I don't understand," Irene said, sobbing quietly. "Why would you kill Sam?"

"She didn't kill Sam," I said. "He's alive."

Celeste whirled, dragging Irene with her. "What are you

doing here?" She placed a knife against Irene's throat. "Stay back."

"I came for Irene," I said.

Which wasn't a lie. I'd came with the intention to get Irene... I just didn't realize it would be to get her out of a dangerous situation.

"Sam's alive?" Irene sniffed. "You're sure?"

I nodded once, my eyes never leaving Celeste's face.

"Why kill Fredrick Longshore?" I asked.

"For Kristi," Celeste said. "She was my best friend. We did everything together growing up. Including ballet."

I nodded as things fell into place. "It was your charm Doc Bowers found on Fredrick's body."

"I didn't realize I lost it until later the next day."

"So you killed Fredrick for Kristi?" I mused.

"Not just Fredrick," Celeste said. "I killed his secretary first. I had to get the job somehow."

"Oh, Celeste," Irene said. "Why?"

Celeste shook Irene. "I told you why! For Kristi! That's what you and Sam never understood. I did it for you guys!"

"We never asked you to," Irene said. "It wasn't your responsibility."

"Kristi's my friend! And when you and Sam took her away and wouldn't let me see her, it broke my heart!"

"You went to work for Fredrick Longshore," Irene said. "How did you expect us to react?"

"Fredrick Longshore was the worst kind of supernatural. He deserved to die!" Celeste said. "I wanted to do that for Kristi. But before he died, I wanted him to pay. That's why I tortured him. I wanted the combination to his safe. He kept enough money in there to pay for Kristi's therapy for years to come. You guys would never have to worry about paying for her care again.

Fredrick owed Kristi that much."

"How did you lure him out to the north side?" I asked. "The witness I spoke to acted as though Fredrick didn't know who was on the phone."

"Distortion spell," Celeste said. "I'm part siren. I disguised my voice and told him I had proof he'd been taking bribes. An offense that could get him disbarred. If he didn't want me going to the police, he'd meet me and bring me money."

"And he believed you?" I said.

Celeste snorted. "Because it's true! He hurried out to where I told him to be, and imagine his surprise when he saw me." She laughed. "Oh, was he angry! Demanded to know what was going on. Threatened to fire me. My great-grandmother has some mermaid magic, and she always keeps enchanted items around her house. A year and a half ago, I took the seaweed and net, knowing I now had the perfect way to ensnare Fredrick and make him pay. She never even missed them. It was at that moment when I stole the enchanted items that my plan started to come together."

"So you ensnared Fredrick and tortured him for the combination to his safe," I said. "Which he obviously didn't give you."

"His heart went out before I could get it!" Celeste exclaimed. "I guess I tortured him a little too much." She tilted her head and stared me in the eyes. "You understand why I had to do it, right? Fredrick *had* to pay. He was a cruel, evil man who got the worst people off for their crimes. He needed to pay for that. He needed to pay for what he did to Kristi."

"*He* didn't run her over," I said. "It was his client."

"It's the same thing!" she screamed at me, waving the knife in the air.

"And Sam?" I asked.

"I needed that charm," Celeste said. "Without it, you might

make the connection eventually. I knew how to sneak into Kristi's room. I'd done it dozens of times when we were kids. I was in her room looking for the charm when Sam walked in. He got mad, demanded to know why I was there, and so I had to shut him up so I could find the charm."

"I heard the yelling and ran upstairs," Irene said. "And I saw it all, Celeste. I saw you stab Sam." Tears fell from her eyes. "Kristi saw too."

"He deserved it," Celeste said. "Both of you deserve to die! You're no better than Fredrick. You both automatically assumed the worst of me when I went to work for that man! You never asked. It took a lot of research for me to find the perfect way to kill his secretary and make it look like natural causes. Did I get any credit for that? No. None! You both just wrote me off. Wouldn't let me see my best friend!"

"You need to put the knife down and step away from Irene," I said. "There's no place for you to go, Celeste. You're done."

"The hell I am." She moved the knife up to Irene's throat. "I'm taking her with me. We're leaving Neptune Oasis. If you let us go, I promise to let Irene go when I get to the mainland."

Smoke suddenly filled the small office, and the smell of something acrid permeated my nose. Because I knew Jace could manipulate fire, I didn't react like I normally would have. Instead, I kept my eyes on Celeste and did my best to ignore the threat of an impending fire.

"What the—"

The second Celeste looked at the heating grate in the wall, I made my move. Shoving Irene to the floor, I tackled Celeste... both of us hitting the ground, the knife clattering to the floor. I came up swinging first. One good hit to her jaw, and she was out cold. Jumping to my feet, I whipped out my Binder and ensnared her in the magical bubble.

"Well done, Detective," Jace said, clapping from the doorway. "I knew you had it under control the entire time."

"Since you sometimes work for PADA," I said, ignoring his praise, "I assume you have them on speed dial?"

Jace smiled. "Perhaps."

"Call them and let them know I'm going to need a transfer, would you?"

"Of course, Detective. It would be my pleasure."

He bent down and helped Irene Stringer to her feet. The woman was sobbing quietly, her heartbreak nearly doing me in.

"Celeste was like a daughter to us," she whispered. "But never would we have wanted her to do this for Kristi."

"Celeste wasn't doing this for Kristi," I said. "She was doing this for her own selfish reasons. She killed a helpless older woman, Fredrick, and nearly killed your husband. It was pure selfishness."

Irene sniffed and nodded. "You're right."

By the time the ambulance arrived to take Irene to the hospital to be looked at and to see her husband, and Nana arrived with my Polaris to transport a ranting Celeste to the station to hold overnight in a cell until a PADA agent could retrieve her… two hours had passed. I hadn't intended for Jace to stay for the entire transfer, but he was insistent.

"I'm exhausted," I said as I closed the bars on Celeste's cell.

Jace nodded. "As am I. Glo is going to be so disappointed she missed all the action."

I snorted. "Raving mad, more like. I'm ready to go home. Dare I ask if I'll see you tomorrow?"

Jace smiled. "Probably not. In fact, Detective, you might not see me for a week or so. Maybe longer. I never know."

I frowned. "What do you mean?"

We stepped outside into the cool October air. It was still nice enough a sweater wasn't needed, and I loved that.

"Let's just say I have one more stop to make."

"Should I ask where?"

Jace didn't say anything…just leaned over and kissed my cheek. "See you around, Detective. Good work today."

❧ 19 ❧

My worst fears were confirmed—PADA was so thrilled with the capture of Celeste Zephyr that they commissioned Jace Solari to be my official civilian consultant. So while I wouldn't have to see him for my daily duties, I would interact with him when a PADA-related case arose.

When Doc Bowers learned she'd mistakenly ruled a death natural causes when it was in fact murder—she'd taken it pretty hard. It had taken Neil, Nana, and me a couple days to rouse her from her depression. Even PADA had assured her there was no way she could have known. The magical drug Celeste had used to kill the secretary left no traces behind.

And what was worse, the fertility stone was still unaccounted for. If I were smart, I'd enlist Jace's help to find the stone. But the truth was...I wasn't sure I could fully trust him.

He'd been silent for a week. Just like he said he might be.

I was curious where he was, but I refused to ask Nana if she'd heard anything. When he wanted to show his face...he would.

I opened the door to Seashell Sweets Bakery and stepped inside, inhaling deeply and savoring the smell of sugar and wheat.

"Hey, Isla," Kyra called out from behind the counter. "Your usual?"

I raised my hand and nodded.

"I'll buy her order," a turtle shifter said.

Even though a week had passed since Celeste was arrested and Fredrick's murder was solved, I still had citizens coming up to me and thanking me for a job well done.

I wasn't used to that. PADA rarely went out of their way to praise an agent for doing their job. It was sort of nice being recognized.

I turned to find a table…and locked eyes with Jace Solari sitting near a window. He smiled and waved me over.

"Hello, Detective," he said. "Nice to see you."

"Is it, though?" Glo asked, lifting off his shoulder and zipping to my face. "I know you're the reason he was down for a week."

"Enough, Glo." The tone was not one I'd ever heard Jace take with Glo. "I make my own choices."

Glo narrowed her teal eyes at me before flying back to Jace's shoulder.

"Have a seat, Detective," he offered.

Not sure what he was up to, I sat.

"Where have you been?" I asked.

Before he could answer, the bakery's front door opened, and Miranda Warner barreled through the door, her pink and purple tutu floating around her hips.

"Hi, Mr. Jace!" She waved enthusiastically before running over to us. "Hi!" Suddenly shy, the little girl turned to the side. "I'm going to class *again* today."

"I'm glad to hear that," Jace said.

He looked across the room and smiled at Margo Warner. "You tell your mom I said hello. And I can't wait to see you at your recital next month."

"I'm playing a turnip!" The little girl twirled excitedly.

"Miranda," Margo called. "Come pick out your treat."

"Bye!" The little girl waved at Jace and ran away.

"What's that about?" I asked.

Jace smiled. "Let's just say Donald Warner finally stepped up and will not only be paying his wife and daughter a fair and timely child support payment, but he's also chipping in for anything else his daughter might have her heart set on learning."

My eyes widened. "Did you do that?"

He shrugged. "Maybe. Maybe not."

I couldn't help but wonder *why* he would do that. He didn't gain anything from it. Surely the jaded demigod didn't actually have a heart underneath all that arrogant exterior? Which made me wonder about something else.

"I saw Irene Stringer in town yesterday," I said.

"Did you now, Detective?"

"Yes. Irene *and* her daughter. You know, the one who last week couldn't walk. Kristi is now going on short outings with her mom."

He arched an eyebrow. "You don't say."

Glo's scales and wings glowed red...but she didn't say anything.

"Here you go, Isla." Kyra set down my large cinnamon-vanilla latte and an orange-cranberry madeleine. "Are you free tonight? I thought maybe we might go for a night swim."

"I'd love that." I picked up my coffee and smiled. "Say, ten?"

"Perfect. Gotta run. See you tonight."

I watched her walk away and picked up my madeleine. "I better get to the station."

"Glo and I will walk you out." Jace stood and Glo flew off his shoulder. "We have a few things we want to…track down today."

I narrowed my eyes. "You better not be looking for the fertility stone, Demigod."

He spread his arms wide. "Now, Detective, what makes you think that?"

"Yeah," Glo said, her scales glowing green and purple. "What makes you think that?"

Sighing, I waited for him to open the door and stepped outside. Samhain was only three days away, and I still needed to pick up some last-minute items.

"I mean it," I said. "PADA partner or not, I *will* arrest you."

"I would expect nothing less," Jace said.

"How was your rave party last week?" I asked Glo.

"Kicking. There's another one tonight."

My pulse raced. This was perfect timing.

"Really?" I mused. "Are you going?"

"Of course I'm going," Glo snapped. "Didn't you just hear me say it was kicking?"

I barely refrained from reaching up and squishing the moody little dragon between my thumb and pointer finger. Ignoring her, I looked at Jace.

"I was thinking about that dinner you mentioned," I said.

"Were you?" he mused.

"What dinner?" Glo demanded. "I wasn't aware you two were going out to dinner now. What's next? Picking out china patterns?"

Jace chuckled. "Simmer down, Glo."

Glo's scales burned red, and she glared at me. "Our house isn't big enough for two women."

"It's *dinner,* Glo," I said. "Rein it in."

Glo dropped down onto Jace's broad shoulder and continued to glare at me.

"Anyway," I said. "Maybe, if you aren't doing anything, I could stop by tonight?"

"Why do I get the feeling there's more to this than me making you dinner?"

I laughed, but even to my own ears, it sounded shrill and forced. "Don't be so paranoid. You offered to make me dinner, and now I'm taking you up on it."

"Okay. Say seven? I know you're swimming with Kyra at ten."

I smiled and stopped at my Polaris. "Seven sounds great. I can look up your address in the app I have. Should I bring anything? Maybe something to drink?"

"Sure." He eyed me speculatively, and I could tell he thought I was up to something. "See you at seven, Detective."

J ace's house was exactly what I'd expect a bachelor's pad on an island to look like. More hut than house, thatched roof, myriad windows, rocking chairs on the wooden front porch, and dozens of stringer lights around the porch and entire house. Even his palmetto tree in his front yard had lights wrapped around the base.

He was sitting on the front porch, beer in hand, when I strolled through the gate.

"Why am I not surprised by any of this?" I gestured around me. "It screams you."

He stood and grinned. "You think?"

"Yes. It screams arrogant, self-assured demigod."

Jace threw back his head and laughed. "Is that so? Well, I hate to burst your bubble, but the house was fully furnished when I moved in."

"It was?"

"It was." He opened the screen door. "C'mon in, Detective. I just have to put the shrimp on and dinner is ready."

I followed him inside the house and was glad to see the nautical theme flowed from the outside to the inside. It was an open-floor concept, with the living room and kitchen blending together.

In the living room, a coral colored sofa sat against one wall. There was also a driftwood coffee table, palm blade ceiling fan, and a cluster of water-themed pictures framed on a wall.

The kitchen's white shaker cabinets stood out against the sea-glass backsplash, but paired nicely with the rattan pendant lights hanging above the countertop. Accent pieces of blue and green dotted the countertops.

But my favorite thing in the room was the hammock chair.

"The previous owner loved hammocks," he said. "There's even one in my bedroom." He waggled his eyebrows. "Care to see?"

I shook my head at laughed. "Pass."

"What did you bring to drink?" he asked, pointing to the pitcher in my hand.

I glanced down at the container and swallowed hard. It was now or never. "It's called Trapped in the Triangle. The bartender at Pirates Paradise made it for me my first night on the island. I had one with my friend Shayla and her husband. They're amazing." I set the pitcher down on the white quartz countertop. "He gave me the recipe."

"That was nice of him." Jace got down two glasses and poured us each a glass. "We can drink these while I cook the shrimp."

I took the glass he offered me and clinked glasses with him.

"To new beginnings," he said.

"Yes," I murmured. "To new beginnings."

I watched as Jace took a drink, and I pretended to take a sip of mine.

"Well? What do you think?" I asked.

"It's good." He smacked his lips together. "Something in it I can't put my finger on."

"I'll bring out the pitcher while you grill."

Jace took the shrimp out of the refrigerator, and I followed him out the back door and onto his deck.

"Wow," I said. "I didn't realize your backyard emptied out into the ocean. It's gorgeous."

More stringer lights were strung along the back and up two of the trees, giving me a majestic view of the water less than ten yards away.

"Private beach for a mile," Jace said as he dumped the shrimp onto the already hot platter on the grill. "I hope you like mango shrimp tacos."

"I do." I topped off his glass. "There's a lot here."

He gestured to my cup while he flipped a shrimp. "Are you trying to get me drunk, Detective?" He picked up the glass and took a large gulp. "Because I'll let you."

I rolled my eyes and looked out across the water. It unnerved me when Jace flirted with me. Mainly because I didn't want to enjoy it...but I did.

I brought my drink up to my lips and almost took a sip... before I remembered. I needed to keep a clear head if I was going to do what needed to be done to acquire the gold coin for PADA. "Are we eating on the back deck?"

"I usually do, if that's okay with you?"

"Perfect. Want me to bring out the mango salsa?"

Jace smiled. "Sure. And some plates." He took another drink from his glass. "I'll stay here and drink this yummy drink you made and watch the shrimp cook."

I set my glass on the two-person table outside and hurried inside to gather the mango salsa from the refrigerator. If I stayed out there any longer, I'd probably fold and confess what I was up to.

It took me opening three cupboards before I found the plates, but was able to find the silverware on my first try. Hurrying back out, I'd just set the plates on the table when I felt prickling at the base of my neck.

Someone was watching me.

Glancing down the beach, I almost cried out when the same lone figure I'd seen last week stood on the shoreline watching me.

Jace must have sensed something wrong. "What is it, Isla?"

I couldn't tear my eyes away from the figure.

"Isla?"

"Nothing," I whispered.

"It doesn't seem like nothing."

"I think that's my mother up there."

Jace turned off the grill. "Where?"

He took a step toward me, then stopped. Staggered. Dropped his drink. And stood there, his eyes wide with shock and amusement. He tried to take another step toward me...but he didn't get far.

Before he hit the ground, I scooted a chair under him and held onto his massive shoulders so he wouldn't tip over.

JENNA ST. JAMES & STEPHANIE DAMORE

"Sorry," I said. "I really, really am. This isn't going how I wanted it to."

"Because…of your…mother." One corner of his mouth lifted in a smile. "Not…because you…spiked my drink."

I rolled my eyes. "I doubt it's the first time you've had this happen." I looked over my shoulder to where the woman had been standing, but the beach was now empty. "Damn."

"Serves you…right. Detective."

"I told you I'd get the gold coin back."

"You did. Silverflame Flower?"

"Yep. Where's the gold coin?"

Jace grinned. "Maybe you should…pat me down."

I pursed my lips together so I wouldn't laugh. "Jace Solari. I want that gold coin."

"You know…I'm just going…to steal it back…right?"

"You can try. Now, where is it?"

"Nightstand. Bedroom. I'd offer to…give you a tour…but I'm not…feeling like myself."

I grinned. "I think I can manage." I leaned down and kissed his rough cheek. "Be right back."

I opened the door and tore through the house, looking for his bedroom. It wasn't hard to find. I tried not to focus on the intimate surrounds as I rifled through the bedside table.

Sure enough, the gold coin was there!

Snatching it up, I ran back outside. Jace was still sitting where I'd left him.

"I'm not going to feel guilty," I said, pocketing the coin. "I warned you."

He said nothing…just watched me.

"And I know Glo's going to be mad," I continued. "But that's just too bad."

I looked back down the coastline, but there was no sign of the woman anywhere. Strolling over to the grill, I picked up a shrimp and popped it in my mouth.

"Mmm...it's really good." I bit my lip. "Sorry it had to be like this."

"I had my suspicions."

I narrowed my gaze. "Liar."

Again, Jace just stared at me with his beautiful green eyes.

"I already said I'm not going to feel guilty."

One corner of his mouth lifted again. "So you've said."

I sighed and headed for the back door. "I hate the shrimp tacos will go to waste." I looked over my shoulder. "It really does look amazing."

"Stay."

I snorted. "And be around with the gold coin when the Silverflame wears off. No thanks." I opened the back door, but turned around when he called my name. "Yes, Jace?"

"I'm giving you...this one."

"Yeah, right. I beat you fair and square."

"Did you?"

My eyes met his across the deck. "Yes. I beat you at your own game."

Jace reached out and snatched a shrimp off the grill...and popped it in his mouth! "Word to the wise, Detective. It takes more than a tablespoon of Silverflame to put a demigod down. Plus, it has a distinctive odor and taste. Bet you didn't know that? You didn't disguise it well at all. I let you have this one."

I could hear his chuckle behind me as I flew through his house, sprinted down the front steps, and jumped into my Polaris. I glanced back over my shoulder as I shot backward down his driveway, sure he was hot on my heels...but he wasn't.

He stood in the doorway, grinning, and lifted his bottle of beer in the air. "See you at the office tomorrow, Detective."

* * *

Are you ready for the next book in the Enchanted Waters series? Then click here and get *Haunted Waters*. My Book. Find out what happens when an antiques dealer is murdered, and Isla believes her long-lost mom may be a suspect.

* * *

If you'd like to keep up with what Stephanie Damore and Jenna St. James are doing, then join their collective Facebook group Paranormal Cozy Mystery Coven: https://www.facebook.com/groups/paranormalcozymystery

ALSO BY JENNA ST. JAMES:

The series that caused the spinoff!

Looking for a paranormal cozy series about a midlife witch looking to make a new start with a new career? Then A Witch in the Woods is the book series for you! A game warden witch, a talking/flying porcupine, and a gargoyle sheriff! Check out Book 1, *Deadly Claws:* My Book.

ABOUT THE AUTHORS

About the Authors

Jenna St. James writes in the genres of paranormal and contemporary cozy and romantic comedy. Her humorous characters and stories revolve around over-the-top family members, creative murders, and there's always a positive element of the military in her stories. Jenna currently lives in Missouri with her husband, stepdaughter, Nova Scotia duck tolling retriever dog, Brownie, and her tuxedo-cat, Whiskey. She is a former court reporter turned educator turned full-time writer.

When she's not writing, Jenna likes to visit and explore new places, attend beer and wine tastings, go antiquing, visit craft festivals, and spend time with her family and friends. Check out her website at http://www.jennastjames.com/. Don't forget to sign up for the newsletter so you can get a FREE box set and keep up with the latest releases!

* * *

Stephanie Damore is a USA Today bestselling author known for her captivating cozy mysteries featuring smart and sassy sleuths. With a passion for weaving magic and romance into her stories, Damore's books are perfect for readers who crave a delightful mix of happily ever after and whodunit. For information on new releases and fun giveaways, be sure to visit her Facebook group: https://www.facebook.com/groups/paranormalcozymystery